Craving

~~ Campus Heat Series ~~

M.D. Dalrymple

Craving

Copyright 2021 M.D. Dalrymple

ISBN: 9798475164167
Imprint: Independently published

Cover art and formatting by M.D. Dalrymple

This book is a work of fiction. Names, dates, places, and events are products of the author's imagination or used factiously. Any similarity or resemblance to any person living or dead, place, or event is purely coincidental.

If you love this book, be sure to leave a review! Reviews are life blood for authors, and I appreciate every review I receive!

Love what you read? Want more from Michelle? Click the image below to receive Gavin, the free Glen Highland Romance short ebook, plus two more free ebooks, updates, and more in your inbox.

Find the link to sign up at this website:

https://linktr.ee/mddalrympleauthor

Craving

Table of Contents

Chapter One

THE KEY STUCK in the door.

Peyton jiggled it, scraping metal on metal, but the lock didn't budge.

What the hell?

She yanked the key out and looked at it, then bent to peer into the lock. The key looked like it should work — why didn't the freaking thing turn?

Peyton tried the key again, grumbling a string of curses under her breath when it didn't turn.

She leaned her forehead against the cool metal door and dropped her leather attaché case between her feet.

Her first day on this assignment, *her first day!* And this was what she got. A busted lock on a windy day when all she wanted was to get inside her new office and sip her probably now-cold coffee.

Tugging her coat tight to her neck, she brushed wild strands of ash blonde hair from her face where the wind kicked it up.

This was Southern California, not Sacramento. It was supposed to be hot here. Why was this wind so cold?

And why won't this key work?

She dug into her purse, found her phone, and opened the internet app. She pulled up the website for Mount Laguna College and searched for something, anything, that might help her get into the Winters faculty office building.

When she had been tasked with coming down to So Cal to evaluate educational needs, immigration, the number of students coming into colleges, and all of these policies and programs that the state was trying to start or continue or improve, Peyton thought she would be in an office in a local city hall or in a small business complex. That the California Department of Education set her up at a college campus initially surprised her. Peyton soon realized the benefit of that decision, though. It made sense — if she were writing and reporting on educational opportunities and programs for students, then she should probably be in a place where they offer educational opportunities for students.

President Anderson had shown her around MLC the week before, and the campus had bustled with students preparing for finals. Then he took to her office, which was a boring gray building that didn't match the rest of the buildings on campus. Obviously built in a rush to try to accommodate the burgeoning number of students attending college, it resembled a prison more than a college.

Unlike the rest of the campus, which was done in a standard desert stucco and shades of beiges, browns, and reds, this building was an unappealing cinder block eyesore, at least as it looked to Peyton, with standard windows and metal doors. No students were on campus on this blustery Saturday, and Peyton had presumed that would be the ideal time to move her materials in, when she didn't have to try to weave in and out to students. She'd also found parking right next to the walkway up to the building and planned to set up her desk in her office on a quiet Saturday before finals.

If only she could get into the stupid building.

Her phone had the facilities website pulled up with their phone number on the page. She poked it with her finger, so her phone app dialed facilities. A gruff voice on the other end of the line answered on the third ring. Peyton asked if there was a problem with the doors or if she needed another key to get into the Winters' building.

"Can you let me in?" She ended with a plea.

The gruff man indicated that they were on the far side of campus working on the athletic fields and wouldn't be able to help her for at least twenty minutes.

"Twenty minutes?" Peyton squealed into the phone. "What do you mean twenty minutes! It's cold and windy and I have a key that doesn't work. Why can't I get in?"

The desperation in her voice was obvious. Surely this man had to hear it.

The man on the other end grumbled an answer and told her again he'd be there in about twenty minutes.

"Wait, wait, wait," she said. "Is there anything else I can do? Is there anyone else who might be able to help me?"

The man grumbled a little bit *again* and then told her that if she were really desperate, she could always call campus security. They also had keys to all the doors on campus. Then he hung up abruptly without a goodbye. Peyton stood there in shock for a moment, staring at her phone.

Rude.

So far, her day had quite an inauspicious beginning, and if this was the start of her assignment down at Mount Laguna College, she wasn't very excited for the rest of her time here. And that reminded her of another issue, or rather a fight, she'd had with her supervisor. The assistant director had told her it was at least a six-month assignment. That would give her the tail end of the fall semester and all the spring semester to do her research, and then an extra month to write up a report.

Six months? Half a year?

So, she'd had to displace herself, sublease her apartment up in Sacramento, leave her friends, and find an apartment in Southern California that would take her *and* her cat. Initially, the idea of going to the southern half of the state for a short time had seemed like a fun idea, a vacation. Now Peyton wasn't happy about this assignment, no matter how important her boss had intimated it would be. She'd had to uproot everything and be a six-month transplant.

And now she couldn't even get into her office.

The wind picked up, biting at every opening in her coat, and she knew her coffee was now cold — it was probably covered in a layer of brown ice. With a shiver, she swept her finger across the screen on her phone, searching for a campus security link. She found the website with the number, tapped it with her finger, and the phone rang. This time it picked up on the second ring and the voice on the other end sounded considerably nicer than the gentleman who'd picked up at facilities.

"Campus security. What's your emergency?"

Peyton paused for a moment. *A key that wouldn't unlock a door? Not exactly an emergency.*

"Yes, hello. I'm sorry for calling but facilities told me I should contact you. My name is Peyton Clark. I am new on campus. I have an office here at the Winters building, and my key doesn't seem to be working, and I've been standing in the cold for a little while." She hoped that the mention of standing in the cold might earn her some pity points with whomever it was on the phone.

"Yes, ma'am. Actually, we do open doors quite often for professors and administration. Let me head on down your way. Give me about two minutes. My building's on the other side of yours."

A shocking flash of warmth amid the cold air suffused through Peyton. At least *this* person was being nice to her, and maybe he'd help her get into the building and get warm.

"Thank you so much. I'm right out front. I'll be waiting. I'm wearing a long gray coat."

"Copy that. I mean, Ok. I'll find you."

Then the phone clicked, and Peyton was once again left to her own devices, loitering in front of the door, trying to pull her coat against the cold.

So much for sunny Southern California.

The man was as prompt as he'd promised, and she had picked her case from the ground when he approached. He was an obviously fit man, only a few inches taller than she was, with a broad chest and muscled arms that fit the long sleeves of his uniform neatly. He had a name tag that read Rivera, and she was grateful that when he walked up, he wore a pleasant smile. His dark hair was cut short with the top brushed over a bit and still somehow managed to shine even in the cold gray day.

"Hello, Miss Clark?" he asked.

Peyton tipped her head and then flicked it at the door. "Yes, hi. I'm sorry. I'm new here, and they gave me this key, and it doesn't seem to be opening the door."

Officer Rivera held out a long-fingered hand. "May I see your key?" he asked.

His voice had a deep, natural rumble. And Peyton thought it warm and welcoming, not at all hard or gruff sounding like she expected a cop's voice would be. She handed over the key. He held it up, his black eyes studying it, and then he handed it back.

"Yeah, this is your office key for your interior office. They didn't give you a key to the main door? A second set of keys?"

Peyton glanced down at her key ring in her hand. "No, I just got this set of keys. I thought it worked both doors. You know how some keys do that?"

Officer Rivera smiled widely, and he chuckled. "Yeah, yeah. I've seen that like doors in houses. Here, we have a little bit more security. You'd be surprised how many people want to break into the offices in the buildings on a college campus."

"You're right. I'd probably be surprised because I can't imagine anyone wanting to," Peyton said. "Is that a problem and campuses especially here? Or in California in general?"

Officer Rivera shrugged as he pulled out a giant key ring from his belt and fiddled with the keys.

"I don't know about other schools, but here on campus, we have anything from thieves to dumb kids playing a prank. So we have added security. We've been working on adding more cameras," he pointed quickly to the roof of the building, "and we started using a two-key system for most buildings."

Peyton made a mental note of this information. She wasn't sure if it would be useful at all with her paperwork or her report, but the idea of added security with more students was probably something that needed to be addressed by the department.

"Are you going to be able to get a main set of keys?" Office Rivera asked as Peyton flipped her head back to him, realizing she'd let herself get caught up in her thoughts again. It was a bad habit she had. Many times, people thought she wasn't paying attention, but really she was deep in thought with some other idea that had grabbed her focus.

"I'm sure I can talk to President Anderson on Monday," she answered. "Will the door self-lock when I leave? Otherwise, I won't be able to lock the main door when I leave here today."

Officer Rivera's dark eyes studied her intently. "I'm sorry. I don't know who you are. And I know most of the faculty. Are you a visiting professor? Why're you here on a

Saturday before finals?"

The kind tone was still present, but it had a slight edge of inquiry and command. *Ahh, there it is. The officer wants to make sure he's not letting one of those thieves into the building.* Peyton had to stop herself from laughing and bit at the inside of her cheek.

"Oh, I am so sorry," she said. "My name's Peyton Clark. I'm with the Department of Education, and I've been assigned to Mount Laguna College for the next six months to study the impact of the number of students on our college system to see what type of programs we either need to add or improve to help serve students."

She cringed inwardly at her answer — she sounded like a recording.

Officer Rivera's soft, dark eyes widened. "Well, I hadn't expected that answer." He gave her another wide smile. "And Mount Laguna College was picked for this? Shouldn't you be at, like, a government office?"

Peyton nodded, her blonde hair whipping in the wind. "Yeah, I thought the same thing, but it makes sense. If I'm studying the impact on colleges, I should probably be *at* a college."

Officer Rivera crossed his arms over his chest into a more relaxed stance and nodded.

"Yeah, that makes complete sense. It'd be difficult to study what's going on in the colleges if you weren't on a college campus. Should Mount Laguna feel fortunate that we were selected for this noble assignment?"

At this, Peyton did burst out laughing, and Officer Rivera's face brightened as he smiled along with her.

"Here," he said, "let's get you inside and out of this wind. We'll make sure the key to your office works. And then, since you're new here, are you moving stuff in? Do you need help getting things from your car?"

She nodded as he unlocked the door and opened it wide, and the thrust of warm air from inside the office hit her like a wall. She'd never been so grateful for central heating in her life. She scrambled inside, and Officer Rivera followed her in, closing the door against the wind behind them.

"What office are you?" he asked, extending his hand to lead her down to the hall.

"It's the main floor, 110," she answered, and he stepped in front of her, his police belt jingling as he let her down to the office near the end of the hall.

"Give your key a try and let's make sure that one works."

Peyton slipped the key in, and it turned like butter. A rush of relief coursed through her that at least one thing went right this day. She glanced up at Officer Rivera's smiling face. *Maybe two things.*

"Well, I do have some boxes in my car, but I don't wanna keep you if you have stuff you need to do," Peyton told him as she set her attaché case and her purse on the banged-up metal desk in the middle of the room.

Officer Rivera waved his hand at her. "No, you're good. My partner's back at the main office. I've got my radio if there's a problem, and I'd hate to have you lifting heavy boxes in this wind by yourself. Many hands make light work."

Peyton liked that comment — it settled on her like a comfortable blanket, cliché as it might have been. Sometimes those old sayings were spot on.

"Officer Rivera, *that* is an amazing offer. I'm so grateful that I got a hold of you today. You've been much more helpful than facility services."

At this, he laid a hand on that broad chest and belly-laughed, a rich rumbling that reached Peyton's core.

"That's not saying much," he answered. "Most of the time, we're lucky if we can get facilities to do anything. All they seem to do is ride around on their little golf carts. Are you ready to go get the rest of your stuff?"

Peyton nodded, and once again he led her out the door, holding the main door open against the wind, and she walked him to her car.

"Thank you again, Officer Rivera," she told him.

"Mateo," he said, his voice like butter. "My name is Mateo."

Had she missed how fitted his navy-blue uniform pants were as they clung to his backside when he walked in front of her? Of course not. Or how fit and how cut he looked in the uniform? Of course she had. Her relationship status was one of the reasons this temporary move down here had been so easy. How long has it been since she had a date? A real date? More than meeting someone for coffee at a random coffee shop and then going home by herself? Peyton couldn't answer that question. In all honesty, as much as she hated to admit it, more than a year? Longer than that?

Her friends had told her that she worked too hard, that she needed to take some time for herself, go on a date, have some fun, let loose a little bit. Peyton had always been more of a straight-laced, down-to-business kind of woman. Other than hanging out with friends every once in a while, she hadn't really dated or taken time for herself with anything. No trips, no days at the spa, nothing but work and home and her cat. And at home with her cat usually meant more work.

This small tête-à-tête with Officer Rivera, or rather Mateo, might not exactly be *me* time, but for Peyton, it was the exact kind of connection she needed, being some newbie on an assignment in a new town where she didn't know anybody.

As they carried boxes of files from her car, Officer Rivera had tried to call her *Miss Clark* again, but she corrected that quickly.

"You can call me Peyton," she told him.

Mateo tipped his head down to her. He brought the boxes into her office and helped her move the desk so it didn't dominate the center of the room. He even went into an empty office used for storage and brought out a couple of chairs and another filing cabinet. She joked that he was quite the procurer.

He winked at her, *winked at her.* "Your wish is my command. Is there anything else I can procure for you?"

He probably meant it as a joke, but Peyton really needed a new cup of coffee. She glanced at the cold one sitting on the edge of her desk and flicked at it with her finger.

"Do you know anywhere to get a fresh cup of coffee around her on a cold Saturday?"

Mateo's eyes shifted away from her. When his eyes returned, they were bright and eager.   "Because it's getting near finals, I don't think the cafeteria is open. We can check, but then you might be drinking cafeteria coffee," he said with a slight grimace. "But we have a decent coffee pot at the security office. It even has flavored coffee options in the little cups, so I can make you a mean hazelnut mocha if you're interested."

Peyton pounced on his words — they were like magic. A fresh cup of coffee that wasn't cafeteria fare? When he asked the question in his light tone, far too light for what she expected from a police officer, Peyton realized he might be flirting with her. But she slammed that idea down in her head.

No, you're desperate because you haven't had a date in over a year, she told herself. *He's not flirting; he's being a nice guy to the new kid on the block.*

She grabbed the old cup of coffee and tossed it in her new waste bin at the side of her desk.

"I would love a hazelnut mocha," she answered.

Chapter Two

WHAT AM I DOING? Mateo asked himself.

He tried to logic it out, tried to tell himself he was only being a great campus police officer, helping someone in need. He was contributing to the campus community, which was a lot more than Aaron ever did. If the guy managed to show up one day *not* drunk, that alone would be a miracle. Helping someone on campus? For Aaron, that was like asking for the moon. Mateo had left him in the office, knowing that it would've been useless to send Aaron to help someone get into the building — worse than sending facilities in their little golf carts.

But the woman had sounded desperate on the phone, he thought as he walked her over to the security office, and he was always opening doors for faculty. When they forgot their keys and couldn't get a hold of facility services or if they didn't have a key for that building . . . There were any number of reasons why he was opening doors on campus, but in truth, he normally popped over, unlocked it with a wave, and left. But this time — coffee? With an attractive blonde?

This young woman with her shoulder-length, blonde hair whipping around her face, standing shivering in the cold, triggered something in him that his brother Damon would laugh over.

Damon thought Mateo's heart was too big for his body, and as a police officer, Mateo should really be thinking with his brain. Mateo understood Damon meant it as a compliment. He was saying Mateo was a nice guy. And especially in the heated environment today where cops weren't well liked, Damon had once told him that it was men like Mateo who made all the difference and really helped others. On bad days or days where Mateo felt like he wasn't making a difference, he kept his brother's words in his head and close to his heart.

For the first time in a long time, today felt like one of those days. It had been relatively quiet on campus over the semester. He'd broken up one small fight in the beginning of September and a few acts of vandalism this month, but other than escorting people to their cars at night or unlocking doors, really he'd been a little more than a bellman for the campus. Here he was once again helping someone new to town move into a new office. If that was all that happened today, Mateo considered it a good day.

He actually hoped that Aaron took a call while Mateo was out helping Ms. Clark, because he had a sinking sensation that Officer Green was not going to make as strong an impression as Mateo might. Especially if this woman had something to do with the Department of Education, having someone like Officer Green meet her might not bode well for Mount Laguna College. Mateo didn't know exactly what her job was, but the last thing he wanted to do was to give someone who had influence on where their money came from a bad impression.

Luck was on Mateo's side. When he opened the door to let Peyton into the campus security office, Officer Green was nowhere to be found. He might have been on a call or hit the head. Mateo didn't know and didn't care.

"Come on in," he said, opening the interior door so Peyton could enjoy the heat as she waited for her coffee.

She scanned the inner office as she entered.

"Ohh," she said, "I get a peek at the inner workings of campus security. I feel lucky."

Mateo chuckled lightly at her joke and walked over to the coffee pot. He grabbed two large cups with plastic lids and waved a hand in front of the selection of flavored coffee pods, feeling a bit like a spokes model on a game show.

"We have quite a selection, surprisingly," he told her. "Which do you prefer?"

She peered at the different offerings and pointed to the one in green.

"Irish cream sounds delicious. Can you make it extra hot, and do you have sugar?"

Mateo popped the pod in and started the coffee pot. Then he pointed to the sugars.

"We have a whole selection of those as well."

Peyton grabbed a few and a little creamer cup and grinned at Mateo with a grateful smile.

"Thank you very much for this. I was really feeling kind of down at the door when it wouldn't unlock. It's cold and my coffee was getting cold and nobody was here." She was rambling, yet he nodded to show he was paying attention.

As she spoke, he flipped the warm coffee cup out from under the coffee pot and handed it to her. She blew on it, her bright pink lips forming a pucker. Everything about her appeared rather bright to Mateo. He wasn't sure if it was because the day was so gray or that she was someone new, but between her super light hair, her skin that was oddly pale for Southern California, and the bright pink lips that matched her fingernails, Peyton exuded a sense of brilliance.

Maybe that was a positive way to look at it — particularly if she were evaluating the college.

"Well, this coffee is a sight better than anything you'll get at the cafeteria. The students have been pushing to get one of those trucks from the local coffee shop or cart or something, but the school hasn't managed to negotiate anything. Because it's probably not high on their list of concerns."

Hint hint, Mateo thought to himself.

Peyton closed her wide blue eyes as she sipped her coffee, like she was tasting perfection. She was a rather animated woman, and between the way she tended to ramble on or the way she looked at things as if she were evaluating everything as quickly as she was seeing it, Mateo was enthralled. He was grateful that he'd picked up this Saturday morning shift.

"I should get back to the office," she told him. "I have some unpacking to do, and I'd like to get settled in so when I show up on Monday everything is ready to go."

Mateo nodded and snapped his lid on his own cup of French roast. "Let me walk you there. If you want the front doors locked while you're in the building, I can do that for you so nobody else comes in, if that's a concern you have. If it's not a concern," he shrugged and tipped his cup to sip the coffee, "and it probably isn't because there's nobody here on campus today. It's pretty empty and we haven't had any major issues this whole semester. I can leave it unlocked and then you can call me when you get ready to leave. I'll come back and lock the door for you. At least until you can get your own set of exterior door keys."

She grinned over her cup of coffee, her ocean-blue eyes flashing at him. *My God, she is an attractive woman,* he said to himself and then cleared his throat. This was work — he worked with her on campus. He shouldn't be thinking this way about someone he was supposed to be helping. He knew better than that, yet those eyes . . .

"I would love to have you walk me back. Dr. Anderson walked me around campus and showed me some things, but if there's any additional places I might need to know, any secrets,

I'd love to hear them. Especially the best place to park for my building when it's really busy during the semester, and how busy my building gets, so I know the louder and quieter times of day."

"At your service, ma'am," he said, giving her a mock salute and opening the door to let her out into the brisk air .

When Peyton got home that afternoon, the first thing she did was pick up her cat — the fat orange tabby that was meowing at the front door when she entered her apartment — and brought him into the bedroom with her. He was such an attached, lovely thing, and she was grateful for at least a little bit of company.

Moving to a place where she didn't know a single soul had been daunting. No family for friends . . . Then she smiled to herself as she whipped her ash blonde locks into a messy ponytail. Where she didn't know anybody wasn't quite right. Her brief interlude over coffee with Mateo had been a welcome reprieve to her morning, but as soon as she was in her office, she forgot about everything else, as she tended to do, and got busy organizing her files and setting up her task list for the upcoming week. It was after three by the time she was done and felt she was in a place where she could stop. She had rung Mateo, who had arrived promptly to lock the main door.

She changed into her sweatpants, and as she hung up her dress pants in the closet, she reached into the pocket and pulled out the card Mateo had given her. On the front side, it was a standard business card from the school with his name emblazoned in blue — blue, gray, and white were the school colors. But then he'd flipped it over, taking a pen from his breast pocket and clicked it. With all the efficiency she expected from a police officer, he'd written on the back of the card.

"Here. In addition to the information on the front, I'm giving you my cell phone number in case it's after hours and campus security isn't answering the phone. In case you ever have a problem on campus or need a door unlocked," he paused and gave her a wicked grin, "you can call me. I live close to campus, so it's not a big deal. I typically work Tuesday through Saturday from eight until five, but I do work a lot of overtime so you can usually find me on campus."

Then he'd handed her the card, gave a slight bow from his tight midsection, and left her at her car. She had enjoyed the view as he walked off back toward the police office.

She couldn't necessarily call Mateo a friend, but at least she knew someone other than the president of the college. And it was nice to know that if she did have a problem on campus, she knew immediately who to go to. That relieved some weight from her shoulders so she could focus on her larger task at hand.

Once she was comfortable, she lifted the cat again and brought him into the kitchen with her. She poured him a small bowl of food and refreshed his water, then popped a frozen meal into the microwave. She poured herself a glass of sparkling water, and once the microwave dinged, she took it all into the small living room where she opened her laptop. She also turned on the television to some brain-dead reality TV as background noise as she got back to work for the evening.

Her fat orange tabby, whom she had aptly named Marmalade, jumped onto the couch and curled up right beside her as she lost herself in her work.

Chapter Three

PEYTON HAD SENT an email to President Anderson letting her know she needed a new set of keys for the main door of her prison-like office building. Until that happened, Peyton hoped when she arrived on Monday morning that facilities had already come around and unlocked all the doors to campus. It was finals week, and Peyton had already reviewed the website and noted that many finals started at 7 a.m. on Monday, so she assumed she'd be able to get into the office building with no problem. She had a nuance of sadness at that thought. She would've liked to call Mateo, see his darkly smiling face again, but then she recalled he'd written on his card that he didn't work Mondays so she wouldn't see him, anyway.

The campus was a sight busier on Monday morning when she arrived than it had been on Saturday, but not nearly as busy as it had been the week when she toured with President Anderson. Students were serious about taking their finals and leaving campus as soon as possible.

Peyton recalled her own time as an undergraduate and graduate at the University schools in California. Finals week was always a light week — get in and get out. The most boring week on campus.

She unlocked the door to her office and settled in before going over her task list. Peyton lived by her checklists — she was so scatterbrained at times, she had to write everything down, which was an odd contrast to the strange focus she could then lose herself in at other times.

Contacting several program heads at MLC and other campuses before they left for break topped her list. Her chicken-scratch handwriting listed whom she needed to email, and as she set up her email group list, a knock came at her door. President Anderson peeked her head in.

"Ms. Clark, I'm so sorry about the key mix-up," she said, placing a shiny new key on the corner of Peyton's desk. Peyton waved her off and tucked an ash blonde lock behind her ear.

"Don't worry about it. I got in and got settled just fine."

Dr. Anderson looked around her office as she tugged on the bottom of her smart-fitting blazer. Peyton had brought in a plant that morning and some framed photographs, including one of her cat. She had worried it might make her look like a crazy cat lady, but really, she didn't care. This assignment was for only six months.

"It looks good in here." The President's eyes flicked to the chairs and the file cabinet. "Did someone help you move in? This seems like a lot of work for one person."

Peyton nodded as she stood up to hand a file to Dr. Anderson. "Yes, I was lucky one of your police officers was on campus and was able to get me in. Then he helped me arrange the furniture so I could start off today with a bang." She smiled at Anderson, who nodded in response.

"Oh, okay. Good. We've had no issues with our police officers. In fact, ours are well-liked. I want our students to feel safe on campus. We're fortunate we haven't had a lot go on this past semester, but we do have a break coming up. You never know what the future is going to hold."

Peyton nodded again. "The officer was very professional and very helpful. From what I see, it looks like you've got a good team. And I like how you acknowledge concerns in regard to students and campus security. Not that it's necessarily on my list of programs, but the idea of helping students feel empowered and be successful, well, many factors come into play. Having officers like the one I met on Saturday is really helpful. Do they have any special training for working with college students or working on a campus or are they just security?" she asked.

Might as well start digging into the idea of what I'm here for.

Dr. Anderson touched the file under her arm. "They're full police officers recruited from different policing organizations, from police academies and the like. We offer a salary comparable to police officers in other towns across the state. They do have to take special training and professional development on dealing with students, on working on a college campus, and the issues that go along with that. Then there's training to deal with disadvantaged students as well, so they go through a decent amount of training to have a job on the campus."

Peyton grabbed a pad of paper and a pen offer desk and jotted down some notes as the president detailed policing on campus.

"Thank you for that, Dr. Anderson. That's really useful with regards to what kind of programs and services and policies we need to make on college campuses. I appreciate you being open with me about it." Sounding sweet might encourage the colleges to be more forthcoming, something Peyton's boss had encouraged, and as her mother always said — you catch more flies with honey than vinegar.

"The more we can do to help our students be successful, the better it is for everybody. I want to make sure we're offering the best academic experience to our students as possible."

Peyton nodded as she wrote. "Would it be possible for me to get a list of those trainings or a schedule of the professional development so I might add it to my report at the end of the semester?"

Dr. Anderson dipped her head, her thinning hair falling in her face a bit. "I'm an open book, Ms. Clark. If you need anything, just ask."

"Awesome." Peyton smiled widely at Dr. Anderson.

She hadn't realized how threatening she might appear to the administration, and then she wondered if that was why Mateo had been so nice to her the other day. What did the Department of Education tell the staff regarding her presence here? Did they think she had some sort of pull in their funding, or that they might lose funding if she didn't like what she saw?

"And Dr. Anderson," Peyton offered as a way to mollify her, "I'm looking for any of those concerns, just for program evaluation. That's it. Anything I do here today or for the next semester doesn't reflect on Mount Laguna College or your funding in that larger sense. This is just where I'm stationed. I'm going to be looking at a bunch of Southern California colleges, and we're only looking at ways to make programs better. Nothing I do or review will cut funding."

The look of relief that washed over Dr. Anderson's face struck Peyton as absolutely hilarious, and she had to bite her tongue so she didn't laugh out loud at the poor woman. She probably should have said those words the very first time she'd met with the President. Why hadn't she thought of that? Of course, Peyton was focused on everything at the college, trying to figure out where she was moving, and all the work she had to complete over the next six months that she hadn't realized this poor president might think she was coming in to cut funding. *Oh, the poor woman.*

"Well then, Ms. Clark, I'll leave you to get to work. Anything you need, again, you ask me, and you'll have it in an instant. Our school is at your disposal."

Peyton smiled widely one more time and waved as the president left. As she leaned back at her desk, she thought again about her cup of coffee with a security officer on Saturday, and a flare of sadness burst in her chest. He'd probably only been sucking up to her to make sure he kept his job and MLC's funding. That was a disappointing thought.

Because she had *really* liked Officer Riviera.

Craving

Peyton's day on Monday was so frantic with phone calls and emails that she barely found time to breathe. She got home later than she expected, fed her mewling, protesting cat, and crashed into bed without another thought. She didn't bother to eat or wash her face. All she wanted was her pillow. She'd tackle more box unpacking later.

When her alarm trilled early on Tuesday morning, she rubbed the sleep from her tired eyes, tried to hide the shadows on her skin with a bit of makeup, and made herself an extra-large cup of coffee. Getting ready for another day — with so much information and so much she needed to do – it was daunting. Her mind spun as she tried to collect her scattered thoughts and figure out what she needed to complete for the day.

Peyton walked into her office building, which was again unlocked, then she slipped the key into her own office doorknob. As focused as she was on her mental task list, she didn't notice the tall, steaming cup of coffee on her desk corner until she was actually sitting down.

She paused, slowly setting her bag on the far side of her desk and regarded the coffee cup. Peyton had immediately recognized it — the cup was one from the campus security office.

Officer Rivera must have left it for her only moments ago. It was still steaming.

Biting her lip to hold back a smile, she sniffed from the opening in the cup, and sure enough, the heavenly scent of Irish cream filled her senses. Her smile burst forth. If the police officer was kissing up to her because he thought she was somehow going to affect his position on campus, he was doing a pretty good job.

Dumping her own boring and now cooling cup of coffee in the trash, she grabbed the Irish cream coffee and took a long, indulgent sip. The way to a man's heart was supposedly through his stomach, but the way to Peyton's heart was a superb, flavored cup of coffee. Nothing helped her focus more. When she had lifted the cup, she also noticed a few extra sugars on the desktop. She picked up one of them and tapped it against her fingertip, biting at her lips. Who did something like this — a surprise cup of coffee with no note, no text? Something just for her, no strings attached? That was a level of thoughtfulness Peyton hadn't seen in too long a time.

She grabbed her pen and a pad of paper from her desk drawer and quickly wrote down her mental task list so she wouldn't forget as she marveled over the coffee gift. God knew, with how flighty her brain could be and how lost she could get on any single task, writing things down so she didn't forget was an invaluable life hack. Once she made sure she had everything down, she turned to her phone and dialed the extension for campus security. He picked up on the second ring.

"Campus police. How can I help you?"

"Hello. Is Officer Rivera there?" she asked, her heart pounding in her chest. A deep chuckle came from the other side of the phone.

"Hello, Ms. Clark," Rivera said. "I trust you're having a good day on your second day on campus?"

The deep rumble of his voice sent a shiver through her, and even though he couldn't see it, Peyton had to bite back a smile. How did he recall that she'd mentioned Monday was her first day? She was lucky she'd remembered!

"I am having a better day now that I have this cup of Irish cream coffee in front of me," she told him. Again, his gruff chuckle rolled through on the phone.

"I thought that your first day might've been quite busy, and if it went anything like your Saturday, you might need something to help get you started."

Peyton flushed with warmth all the way to her toes at that consideration. "It was unbelievably thoughtful. I haven't had anyone be that thoughtful for me in a long time. I'm a bit of an *all work and no play* kind of person. I can get overly focused on things sometimes," she trailed off a bit.

"No worries," Officer Rivera told her in his deep, confident voice. "I'm sure we can all be like that sometimes."

His positivity was kind, but Peyton knew the real truth. She'd lost friends, angered family, had broken up with men, all because sometimes her focus didn't shift very well. Her doctor had once asked if she'd ever been treated for something like ADHD or autism. Peyton had wondered the same thing, but every test she'd taken, every doctor appointment came back with the same result. She was perfectly fine, she was told; she just tended to get hyper-focused.

Sometimes she wondered if the doctors knew what they were talking about. Because it seemed like she was the only one who got hyper-focused like this, and a lot of other people thought her strange or scatter-brained because of it. The only upside was it helped her remain so fixated on her job that she'd landed this prominent position with the Department of Education. A silver lining, she'd told herself.

"I really appreciate that," she said, her voice tightening. "But you need to know that sometimes I get so focused I don't even know who I'm in the room with. I don't pay attention to people. I can be in the middle of a conversation and . . ." she trailed off again. "So anyways," she continued abruptly, "I really wanted to thank you for the coffee, and I had to do it first thing in the morning before I got focused on something else and completely forgot."

She tried to laugh it off. Why had she opened up about her weird focus issues with the guy who only met once, when he'd done nothing more than be kind enough to bring her a cup of coffee? Peyton huffed. No wonder people thought she was crazy. Officer Rivera, however, appeared to take it in stride. Peyton wondered if that was part of his job requirement. Dealing with people like her.

"Well, with that thought in mind," Officer Rivera continued as though she hadn't given him too much information, "and before you get involved with anything else today, I was wondering if I might meet up with you for lunch. The cafeteria may have horrible coffee, but they do a fair job with their lunch menu since that's the main meal students and faculty eat on campus."

Peyton stopped fiddling with the sugar packet and took another sip of coffee as she collected her thoughts. Was he asking her out on a date? No, no, he couldn't be. It was only her second day officially on campus, and she'd just met this guy. However, of all the ways to go on a date and do it safely, meeting him on campus for lunch might be the best way to go. And truthfully, even if it wasn't a date, if he was being a nice guy, did she really have so many friends in here that she could afford to say no? She did *not*. And if it was lunch with someone who already knew about her and she faded to black or seemed like she wasn't paying attention, the more the better. She grabbed her planner from her bag.

"Just a moment," she said to the phone.

Peyton didn't think she had anything on her schedule as she had only just started at MLC. She didn't recall scheduling any meetings yesterday, but she forgot so often, so it was always better to check. Sure enough, Tuesday was a big empty blank space in her planner, and she smiled into the phone. The thrilling rush that coursed over her surprised her. Peyton felt like an excited little kid getting ready to go to the amusement park, and she wasn't quite certain why she felt like that.

"It looks like I have all day today open, so when do you want to get lunch?"

"Well, I typically take lunch between 12:30 and 1:30, and Officer Green takes over the desk for me so I at least get that hour. Unless there's an emergency that I get radioed in for, I should have the whole time."

Peyton clutched a pen and wrote the time down in her planner so she wouldn't forget.

"Do you want me to meet you at the cafeteria?" she asked as she scribbled.

"I have to walk right by your building to get there," Officer Rivera told her, "so why don't I meet you outside the Winters building?"

It certainly sounded like a date. *Don't jump to conclusions,* Peyton lectured herself. *This is lunch with a friend. An acquaintance.*

"I'm going to put that notification in my phone, and I'll be right outside the Winters building promptly at 12:30."

"Copy that," Officer Rivera told her.

For some reason, a trail of arousal blossomed low in her belly, and she found it a bit difficult to breathe. What was it that seemed so sexy about that phrasing? Then again, Peyton knew there was something to be said for a man in uniform. Even old clichés had a ring of truth to them.

Peyton hung up the phone and immediately opened up the notifications app to set up a reminder alarm at 12:25. Just because she wrote it in her planner didn't mean she was going to remember it.

Her day planner didn't talk to her.

Officer Rivera ducked into the men's room outside the campus security office before he made it to the Winters building. It was a childish thing to do, something that a high school kid would do — checking his appearance before meeting with an attractive young woman. But then, as his brother Damon would've teased, it had been a while since Mateo had done anything remotely like dating. This was his first time for *anything* in a long time, and he thought he should look at least halfway decent.

With his fingers, he'd worked his short hair until it was even and slicked back slightly. He also made sure he didn't have any coffee stains on his uniform or around his mouth. *That* wouldn't look good. He had to keep his full uniform and vest on for lunch, and while it didn't bug him at all — he was used to it — he didn't know what kind of person Peyton was. Some people got uncomfortable around the uniform. However, she did work for the government, so there was a good chance she wouldn't have a problem with the uniform, the vest, the belt, and the rest of his trappings. The good news was, since he worked on campus, many of the faculty and students knew him, and he had a good rapport with them. The only person he really had to worry about being uncomfortable was Peyton. She was the one person he didn't *want* to be uncomfortable.

At least it wasn't raining on Tuesday. It was partly cloudy, but pockets of sunlight burst through the clouds. In So Cal, after a series of wind and rain, the landscape seemed bathed, refreshed, like the wind and rain were mother nature's way of giving desert a really good scrubbing. The colors seem brighter, the landscape sharper, and the sky seemed more azure than it had before finals started. Mateo slid on his mirrored sunglasses as he walked — a Southern California staple of life.

If anything attested to the fact it was a bright and new day, it was the image of Peyton standing in front of the Winters building when Mateo rounded the corner. Her gray coat had been replaced by a shorter lilac blazer that complemented the blonde in her hair perfectly. She looked like a fairy creature from another world. Then he shook his head to refocus, chastising himself.

Mateo, what are you thinking? This is lunch. She's only here on assignment, don't get your hopes up.

Even as he was telling himself those very words, he knew. He was getting his hopes up.

As he approached the building, she turned to him with her wide smile that lit up her face, the quad, and all of Southern California, or so it seemed to Mateo.

Damon would tease him mercilessly if he knew, but this brilliant looking blonde who had stumbled into his life with her intriguing job had somehow managed to ensnare him.

Don't blow this, he said to himself and smiled back as widely as he could.

She didn't have a pair of sunglasses, so she held her hand up to shade her eyes as she greeted him.

"I really appreciate this, Officer Rivera," she said, squinting against the sunlight that had managed to burst through the clouds. "After what you told me about the cafeteria on Saturday, I wasn't sure it was worth the risk for lunch."

Officer Mateo grinned. "Well, any cafeteria on a campus can be hit or miss," he answered. And then he tilted his face at hers. "Don't you have a pair of sunglasses?"

Peyton patted her face. "Oh no, I forgot them. It was gray when I got here. And honestly, I don't even know where they are right now. In some random box, probably."

Mateo's cheek twitched with his grin. Of course, she was from northern part of the state, where it wasn't as sunny as it typically was in the southern part of the state. Down here, people wore sunglasses like they were vampires, worried that their eyes might turn to ash in the sunlight.

"Are you still trying to unpack?" Mateo asked as he started walking towards the cafeteria. Peyton joined him at his side.

"Most of my stuff is unpacked," she answered. "I got here over a week ago, and they gave me some time. And then last week I wasn't doing a whole lot for the job yet, so I was able to get a lot unpacked. But you know how it is when you move. It seems like there's another box, and you always have to lose something."

Mateo agreed. When he had first moved in with his brother Damon, they fought like cats and dogs because Damon had packed some important paperwork and accused Mateo of losing it. Mateo sagely pointed out that they had just moved in, and the paperwork was probably in a box Damon hadn't unpacked yet. Damon had found the paperwork not even a week later.

Then when Mateo had moved out and got his own small, one-bedroom apartment close to campus, he had the exact same problem and misplaced a box of paperwork. He had felt a sudden urge to call up Damon and apologize. Only Mateo had no one to blame for losing his paperwork but himself. That box also was mysteriously unearthed shortly after he'd finished unpacking.

"It will undoubtedly be in the very last box you unpack," Mateo joked. Peyton patted her cheeks again.

"I guess I'll have to find a new pair somewhere else. Do they sell any at the student store?" Her voice sounded disbelieving, as though she already knew the answer Mateo was going to give.

He shook his head. "No, sorry. Just pens and notebook paper and books. And snacks. Lots of snacks at the bookstore if you ever need something."

They arrived at the cafeteria which buzzed with dozens of students. Normally during the semester, hundreds of students visited the cafeteria at lunchtime, but as it was finals week, fewer students remained on campus, which meant fewer students at the cafeteria. Mateo was grateful for that, because otherwise it might have been too loud, or trying to get their food would have been a much more arduous experience.

As it was, he swung open the door, and Peyton walked right in without having to wait in a line. He led her to the buffet where prepackaged salads and a selection of entrees and fruit were packaged for the picking.

Mateo hefted his navy-blue vest to the side to grab the protein plate consisting of chicken on a flatbread sandwich, a hard-boiled egg, and string cheese in one plastic container. Peyton seemed a little unsure, her ice-blue eyes flicking from one salad and entrée to the next.

"Any recommendations? I'm not really sure what to expect when I open the plastic."

Mateo laughed at her assessment. Besides her looks, Peyton had personality pouring out of her. When so many people were closed off and guarded, she was surprisingly honest and open, something Mateo hadn't encountered in anybody, male or female, for a long time.

He pointed to the salads first. "If you like salad," he said, "then the Caesar is probably the best. They put the dressing on the side so the lettuce doesn't get mushy."

Then he pointed over to the entrees. "I like the protein one, so if protein's important to you, that might be a winner. If you want something with a little more flair, they have a chicken parmesan type thing I think is pretty good. Otherwise, they have a really neat turkey sandwich that they called Thanksgiving dinner, and it's got a cranberry cream cheese dressing on it, and it comes with fruit on the side. They also recommend with that one you grab a bag of their sweet potato chips to make it more, I don't know, authentic?"

"Well," Peyton said under her breath and reached for the turkey sandwich recommendation, "I like Thanksgiving dinner."

She gave Mateo a slight side smile. Mateo reached over and grabbed the sandwich for her and then they hit the soda fountain for drinks. Mateo carried their trays up to pay but Peyton put a hand on his arm.

"No, no, no." Her face, normally open and bright, had tightened, and Mateo wondered if he'd somehow overstepped. "I can't let you pay for this. Give me back my food and my drink so I can pay for my own."

Her request went against everything inside Mateo. He'd been raised as a gentleman, which meant if you asked someone to meet you for lunch, date or not, you were probably picking up the tab. He opened his mouth to say that to her, but from the ferocious look in her burning blue eyes, he decided against it. He'd make sure that the next time they met up, she would *know* she was on a date with him.

"My apologies," Mateo told her, handing over her food and drink. "I want you to know that, since I asked you to meet me, I was going to pay for it. That's usually the expectation that people have. At least in my experience."

Peyton's fair eyebrows rose on her head as she balanced her drink on top of her plastic sandwich container and pulled out her wallet. "Well, unfortunately for you Officer Rivera," she said with a slight edge to her voice, "if you're gonna meet me for lunch, you're gonna have to learn that I am anything but what you expect."

Oh, I already knew that, Mateo thought and gave her another wide smile. Her statement made his chest swell. He *liked* the unexpected.

"Well, I'll definitely keep that in mind the next time we meet for lunch," he told her.

She pursed her lips together into a rosy-pink line, as though she was trying not to smile at him, but the corner of her mouth wouldn't let her get away with it and fought against her as it curled. Mateo had a sudden, intense desire to kiss that curl.

She wasn't wrong. This woman was *nothing* like he expected.

Craving

Chapter Four

SO IT WAS a date, Peyton told herself as she carried her food to the table. Her eyes kept flicking to the strong, round curves of his ass underneath his fitted uniform. Did they intentionally design the uniforms to be that tight? If anything, it should be against the law for him to wear those pants. Mateo said something to her, and she missed it.

Crap, she cursed to herself. *I wasn't paying attention.*

She lifted her eyes to his tanned face. He'd pushed his mirrored sunglasses onto his head, so she could see that his deep, black eyes were open, questioning — he had asked her a question.

"Pardon?" she said. "I must've been wool-gathering there for a minute."

"No problem," Mateo said to her in a casual tone. "I was asking if this table was okay or if you wanted to sit somewhere else."

The table was at a transition spot where the set of windows opened up like doors, and they could sit inside the cafeteria but still be exposed to the brilliant outside. It was a clever design and a great way to help get nature inside, which Peyton knew for students was important for mental health. She nodded.

"Oh, yeah. This is great," she said and settled next to him.

They chatted lightly as they opened their food and tore into lunch. Over the course of their meal, several students and a few faculty who were still on campus came by and said hello to Mateo. Each one of them flicked their inquiring eyes at her, and Peyton had to work not to react to those glances. The hour went by too fast for Peyton. She was proud of herself — she'd managed to remain focused on their conversation, not letting her mind slip to think about work or the tasks of her day.

But then, it seemed very easy to talk to Mateo. For all that he wore his uniform, which Peyton noticed fit him as beautifully as it had on Saturday, he was relaxed. And he didn't seem to have any issues or qualms with the fact she'd already zoned out on him once today. Too often, men thought that meant she wasn't interested, and even friends thought it for that matter, and pulled away. Instead, Mateo seemed to lean in, and that was a treat Peyton realized she'd missed for much of her adult life.

Once they were done with their meals, Mateo asked for her cell number, and she readily gave it to him. Then they cleared the table and dumped their lunch garbage into the trash as they left the cafeteria. Mateo continued to chat with her as they walked back towards the Winters building. He asked about her family, her likes, and even her cat. The more she talked to him, the more relaxed she became. How did he calm her every last nerve?

Mid-sentence, however, the radio attached to his vest beeped, and Mateo immediately grabbed it.

"Rivera, copy," he spoke into the radio, his tone shifting from casual and relaxed to one with a hard edge. The radio beeped again.

"Rivera, we got a call that someone was trying to break into one of the offices over in the science center. Meet me over there on alert."

"Copy that," Mateo said into his radio and turned to Peyton. His eyes were hidden by his sunglasses, but his clenched jaw told her he was all business. He rested his hand lightly on her forearm. "I have to go. I'll definitely call you later."

Then he was running off before Peyton could say another word. As she watched him run off, that sexy ass and his long strides, the intense focus that he had now that he was back on duty, spoke volumes. He had that same focus when he got a radio call as she did for much of her life. And he had no apologies, no regrets; it was part of his job and he was out. Maybe that was why her zoning out didn't bug him as much.

Peyton remained where she was, staring until he was nothing more than a navy-blue dot on the horizon rounding the edge of the humanities building. She'd seen movies and heard rumors around different state buildings that too often police officers didn't have a good track record with significant others. That, with the pressures of their job, they couldn't exactly check in throughout the day, and if their significant other called, they might have to ignore the phone call. That sometimes the security officer's focus wasn't where the significant other expected it to be.

And standing there in a shaft of pale sunshine, just a few weeks before Christmas, Peyton had a stunning realization, rather like an epiphany. Someone like Mateo might be the exact type of person for her. Mateo might understand what was going on when her focus went somewhere else.

He said he'd call her later, and he made it seem like lunch might have been a date. Peyton wasn't one for expectations, but as she reentered her office, she really, *really* hoped he'd call her, and maybe next time, if he did ask her out again, she'd let him pay.

Because she hoped it would be a date. She shook her head at that silly notion. Why would she want to date him if she were leaving in a few months?

Still, it was six months, half a year, and maybe they could have fun together before she left.

No one said dating had to be serious.

Mateo bolted across campus to the science center. The science buildings were a new set of modular construction the campus set up when student attendance had exploded. MLC had built the science center with special STEM funding from the state, and the college was rather proud of the facility. This made any break-ins even more problematic, because those buildings housed a lot of expensive equipment.

When Mateo arrived, he found Officer Aaron Green standing near a pile of broken glass, staring at it as though he didn't know what he was looking at.

Fuck, Mateo said to himself.

Mateo knew that look — one he'd come to see on Aaron more over the past several weeks.

"Hey, Green," Mateo said when he arrived. "What do we have going on here?"

Officer Green turned to Mateo who cringed when Aaron opened his mouth to answer. The smell of whiskey was *way* too strong for this early in the afternoon. He'd drunk his lunch. And most likely his breakfast.

"This is the third break-in over the last two or three weeks," Aaron said, trying to sound authoritative. "It doesn't look like they took anything. Or at least that's what the professor who uses this lab the most told me."

Mateo studied the scene. It did look like a smash and grab without the grab.

What the hell is going on? Mateo asked himself.

The uptick in break-ins was problematic. And to know that someone from the California Department of Education was on campus while this was happening made Mateo's skin crawl.

"Do we have any leads?" Mateo asked.

"No," Aaron slurred.

Fuck, Mateo thought again. If anyone else heard Aaron, they'd know that he was drunk. And the man carried a taser, a baton, and a *gun* for Chrissake. He should not be drinking on the job at all. Mateo made a mental note to encourage him once again to get some help for this problem. He hadn't known Officer Green to be a drinker when he'd started the job, so maybe something was going on in the man's life. Either way, Green shouldn't be drinking in uniform.

"What if it's one of those political groups on campus?" Officer Green commented, dragging Mateo from his mental assessment of his partner. "They've been getting louder and more violent at some of their protests, and if they wanted to take that out on the school..." Aaron trailed off.

Mateo glanced at the outside of the building and then tipped his head toward the door. They went inside to survey the damage as Mateo considered Aaron's words, which had merit. With all the craziness that had been going on, some of these political groups had become more vocal and forceful on campus. But with finals, Mateo thought that those behaviors would have died down.

Maybe I was wrong, Mateo thought.

There didn't seem to be anything missing or even destroyed in the building. Just the busted-out window.

"And we don't have any idea who it is? You didn't catch anybody or see anybody around here when you arrived? Nothing on the cameras?"

Aaron shrugged. "No, and the cameras point more to the front door, not these side windows. The only thing here when I showed up was the broken glass. That's why I think they didn't get anything. The alarm went off before he even had a chance to get inside. Do you want to write this up?"

Mateo pressed his lips together because he was afraid if he opened his mouth, he'd regret the words that rushed out. Write it up? *What the hell?* This wasn't even his call. He wasn't the first on the scene. What was he supposed to write up? But knowing Aaron, he'd fuck it up anyway, and the last thing Mateo wanted was to draw attention to the fact that one of the cops on campus might be a problem.

"Yeah, yeah. I'll write up the report," Mateo answered with a bite of acid in his tone.

"Ok, then let's head back to the office. I'll give you my notes," Aaron said as he started walking away. Mateo remained where he stood and watched the man walk off.

"Green, wait!" Mateo called out.

Aaron spun in an unbalanced turn. Mateo jogged up to him.

"Brother, we have to have a talk about what I'm smelling on your breath," Mateo said in a low voice as he surreptitiously scanned the courtyard. God forbid anybody overheard this conversation.

"What smell?" Green asked.

Mateo worked his jaw at Aaron's dumb-ass question. He was really going to try to play dumb?

"You know what smell I mean," Mateo responded in a flat voice. "For a couple weeks now it's been there, and don't think I didn't notice the bottle of whiskey you think you're hiding in your desk drawer. You cannot be on duty on campus around college students when you're drinking. You have a fucking gun, for God's sake."

"Yeah, like I'd ever pull my gun on campus," Green retorted. "This is all baby crime."

"Fuck, that's not the point, Aaron. The point is you can't be drinking and be on duty on campus. Now I told you before, and this time I fucking mean it. Get yourself some counseling, some therapy, some help, some rehab. I don't care what you do. Just get it done. Because I will *not* tolerate this. If I have to report you, I will."

Mateo was nose to nose with Green.

"What the fuck?" Green answered, slighted at the accusation. The sunlight glinted off Aaron's mirrored sunglasses, and Mateo was certain that if he yanked the sunglasses from Aaron's face, he'd see his bloodshot eyes. "What about the brotherhood, the camaraderie? I can't believe you'd do something like that."

Mateo didn't care to have his integrity called into question and crossed his brawny arms over his chest.

"I don't care how you do it, Green." Mateo's voice was hard. "Just do it. Otherwise, this is going to end badly for you. I'm trying to help you, brother."

Green's jaw clenched as he stared down Mateo for several seconds, then he turned again and marched back to the security office. This time, Mateo watched him go. And knowing he was going to have to clean up Green's mess and write this report, and that they had no idea who was committing this series of break-ins, all of it rankled Mateo.

And this day had started off so great.

He followed Green to the office as he radioed facilities for cleanup and made a mental note to call Peyton after he calmed his anger and finished writing the damn report.

Contact information, surveys, and paperwork from the admin and faculty on the Mount Laguna campus started to pour in, and her email dinged nonstop. Peyton spent her afternoon reaching out to the administration at three other major California universities and several smaller colleges from central California down to the border. How had she amassed so much paperwork already? Her bosses up at the capitol must have been onto something when they tasked her with this project. She was praising the glories of the *blind cc* feature of email that enabled her to send out mass responses when her cell phone buzzed.

Peyton's eyes glanced at her planner to see if she had anything written down. Should she be expecting a phone call? And then it occurred to her — it was her cell phone. If she were getting a call from someone on campus or from another college, wouldn't it have come to the office phone? She flipped up her phone and noted the number. It wasn't a campus number. She pressed the answer button, tentatively wondering if someone up at the Department of Education who wasn't on her list was calling her.

"Hello?" Peyton asked, her voice hesitant.

"Hello, Peyton," Mateo's voice rumbled from her speaker phone. "I wanted to call and apologize for running off on you earlier. I wasn't expecting to get a call, but as I mentioned, we've had a couple break-ins. They usually happen over the weekend though, so I don't know what's going on for a Tuesday."

Peyton had to pause and stare at her phone as he spoke. She hadn't recognized the number because she forgot to add his number to her contacts, and as distracted as she was, she hadn't realized it was his number when it rang.

Focus, Peyton!

Considering how flighty she'd been for the day, Officer Rivera was scoring points with her left and right, and she really didn't know what to make of it. When he'd said he'd call, it was in a rushed, casual manner, and she truthfully hadn't expected anything more from him than lunch. But here he was, calling! Who did that? He didn't make her wait. He didn't send her a generic text, which was what everybody seemed to do. She licked her lips as that smile from earlier that tugged at her lips, curling on both sides.

What was Mateo all about? What was it about this guy who she met all of three days ago and made her feel like the star of her own movie? Hell, made her feel like she was an important part of the universe? What was going on?

"Peyton, are you there? Did I lose you?"

Crap.

"Oh, nope. I'm here," Peyton responded quickly, and she was certain he could hear her beam through the phone. "I'm glad you called. I honestly didn't expect to hear from you for a couple days."

"I get that," Mateo said, his voice earnest-sounding. "That seems to be the thing with a lot of people today. That there's some unwritten rule that we should wait before calling again. But to be honest, I think life's too short. I am a cop, and I haven't always worked with the campus police here at MLC. I've seen some stuff go down, and I think life is too short to wait three days before calling somebody you're interested in."

Peyton's breath caught in her chest. His words held such exuberant power. *Who's honest like this?* Other than her overly open self, of course. She tapped her finger on her desk.

"Holy cow, Officer Rivera," she said in a teasing tone. "You just put it out there, didn't you?" She licked her lips again. When she'd moved down here, getting involved with somebody was the last thing on her mind. If he were interested in something short term, maybe a one-night stand, she could understand that. But something about Mateo gave her the sense he might be interested in something more than a one-night stand. Something fun.

"Yeah, I did," he told her unapologetically. "So I wanted to call and ask you out on an official date. Not at the student cafeteria, and one where I would pay."

Peyton burst out laughing.

"Ok, but here's the deal," she said in her laughing tone, "if I ask *you* out, though, I get to pay."

Mateo's low chuckle joined hers.

"I have to admit, there's something to be said for empowerment and getting rid of gender norms. How about next time you ask me? But this time, I'm asking you. On a date. Do you wanna go grab drinks and dinner somewhere this week when you have time?"

Mateo didn't go straight home after work. After locking his vest in the lock box in the trunk of his car, he drove over to his brother Damon's house in the student neighborhood not far from campus. Damon opened the door wide, his black hair slicked back and a bottle of Corona in his hand.

"Come on in. You slumming today?" Damon greeted him with a fist-pounding hug.

Mateo gave a little laugh as he returned the hug and entered his brother's ramshackle rental house. He'd struggled when he'd briefly lived here with Damon. Mateo loved his brother fiercely — they were closer than brothers could ever be, and he'd been excited to live with Damon when they moved out of their grandmother abuela's house. Damon, unfortunately, was the type of kid who couldn't quite seem to land anywhere. Even today, he was wearing the same stained, once-white tank top that was the core staple of his wardrobe. Who dressed like that?

Damon was an aimless sort. He claimed to be a college student but only managed one or two classes a semester, and that was if he attended class at all. He'd taken this past semester off, and though he claimed to be registered for winter term, Mateo had his doubts. Damon partied a little too hard, enjoyed the lack of responsibility a little too much, and Mateo had a sincere struggle with that. Once he'd started at the police station in town before he worked for Mount Laguna College, Mateo moved out to his own place, claiming that his off schedule was going to interrupt Damon and that he wanted to make sure he could keep his own sleep schedule. Damon took it in stride, finding some new roommates and carrying on as he always did. Sometimes Mateo's chest ached when he thought about Damon and how he couldn't quite seem to find himself.

"Hey, man, you want a beer?" Damon asked.

Mateo nodded. It was after six and he was off duty, unlike his shiftless partner. Damon reached into the fridge and pulled out a cold Corona. He popped the cap on the counter and handed the beer to Mateo.

"What brings you here?" Damon tapped his bottle against Mateo's and took a swig of his Corona. Mateo did the same.

"Well, you've been bugging me," Mateo told him, "so I thought I'd let you know that, at least for a little while, you don't have to worry about me."

Damon's face crinkled. "What the hell do you mean by that?"

Mateo gave him a low laugh and stared down at his beer. "I met someone."

Damon's jaw physically dropped, like something in a comic book, and Mateo bust out laughing.

"No shit," Damon said with a touch of awe. "What the hell? I've been bugging you for months, shit more like a year, trying to hook you up, and here you walk in and say you met someone? Who's the lucky girl?"

Mateo returned his gaze to his beer, wondering how much he should tell his brother. Excitement had been building in him since setting up the tentative date with Peyton. He had to share it with someone.

Ever since he'd spoken to her, Mateo had been on a high. And it made him feel kind of stupid, too. He shouldn't be getting his hopes up. That was a foolish, high school thing to do, especially since she was leaving at the end of the spring semester. But something about Peyton . . . He hadn't been able to get her out of his head since he'd met her on Saturday.

"It's just a date," Mateo told him.

"How d'you meet her? Not some seedy bar?" Damon teased.

"Nope. I met her on campus."

Damon's job dropped again. "Holy shit. Please don't tell me you're dating a student."

Mateo scowled at his brother. "No, no, no. I don't have time to play the HR games like that. But she does kind of work for the school right now. The Department of Education is doing some sort of analysis with a bunch of colleges, and she's running that show."

"And what? You randomly saw her and asked her out?" Damon asked.

The slight pitch in his voice irritated Mateo, and he cut his eyes hard and narrow at Damon.

"Ha ha, very funny. No, since she's new, she was trying to get into her office and start moving in, but one of her keys wasn't working. And you know how facilities can be," Mateo commented.

"Yeah, pretty useless. So what, you opened her door and then," Damon winked, "opened her door?"

Mateo punched Damon's shoulder

"Fuck no. Unlike you, I'm a gentleman. I like to have a date first. I've only just met her, but we're meeting for drinks later this week."

Just saying the words made him flush, and he turned his head slightly so his brother wouldn't see him blushing.

"You dog," Damon told him and slapped him on the back. "Well, I wish you all the best, man. I know that the past year has been a bit of a struggle for you with the ladies, and I hope this woman, whoever she is, is worthy of my brother."

Mateo gave his brother a flat smile. Damon might be aimless, but he was the best brother a man could have.

Chapter Five

A CUP OF COFFEE appeared on her desk each morning for the rest of the week.

Such a simple thing, yet Peyton marveled over it every morning, sitting on the corner of her desk as a caffeinated reminder of Mateo's thoughtfulness. She hadn't even gone on a date with him yet.

They set up drinks and dinner for that Thursday night, agreeing to meet at a local wine bar. Peyton almost canceled at the last minute. She studied herself in the mirror and wondered *what the hell* she was doing going out with a guy she'd met less than a week before. Why did it take moving five hundred miles away to meet someone? She had his name, and she knew he worked for the campus as a police officer, but that was it, and with her track record, she really worried about this date. It might not amount to anything, but what if it did? Mateo seemed like a great guy, and she was on borrowed time.

He seemed okay with her flighty nature, but he hadn't seen how bad she could really get when she wasn't paying attention or when something like work consumed her. Mateo seemed to have much better control over his laser-focused attention.

Her hands shook as she decided what to wear — it had been more than a year since her last date. Was she ready for this?

It's just for fun, Peyton reminded herself. *Calm down!*

She raked her fingers through her hair again before she landed on a fitted, black, long-sleeved T-shirt with a pair of black jeans and black low-cut booties. She ripped a brush through her ash blonde bob and added a little more highlighter to her face before deciding that was enough. He'd seen her when she was rough and not made up already, struggling to get into the Winters building, so the bar for her was pretty low. That thought brought a nervous smile to her face.

As she grabbed her purse, her phone chimed. A text from Mateo.

His text was the single best thing she could have received regarding their date.

Are you as nervous as I am? Mateo asked.

She grinned at her phone. There it was — that was all Peyton needed. At least she wasn't the only one going on this date as nervous as hell.

When she arrived at the bar, with its dim lighting and maroon and brown decor, Mateo was already standing at the door. He hadn't gone inside yet.

"Why are you standing outside?" Peyton asked him as she approached the covered entry. "It's chilly."

Mateo didn't look chilly, though. In his long-sleeved white and blue button-down and his own dark jeans, he looked like he could be an advertisement on the back of a magazine selling men's cologne. His cropped, black hair had been brushed back and shone in the subdued lights of the restaurant. In her heeled boots, she was only an inch or so shorter than he was, and he gave her a smile made more brilliant against his tawny skin. How long had it been since she had seen a brilliant smile like his directed her way?

At that moment, Peyton's nervousness about the date evaporated. Something about Mateo, how he looked, how he moved, how he took everything Peyton did in stride, relaxed her. And as her blue eyes caught his rich black ones, caught his dark expression that she wanted to lose herself in, she told herself that this guy might be one to hang onto.

At least for the next six months.

He opened the door for her, and as they walked in together, she caught a whiff of his musky cologne that stirred her insides and made her thighs weak.

The wine bar, fortunately, was relatively empty for Thursday night at the end of finals. They had their selection of seats, and Mateo asked if she preferred one near the bar or in the lushly decorated restaurant itself.

"How about a table in the restaurant itself? That way we have a little more privacy to talk than at the bar."

Mateo's white smile brightened. "Perfect," he said, and their hostess led them to a small table near the window.

Because it was December, less than two weeks before Christmas, the light had already fled from the sky. A multitude of stars twinkled, and Peyton felt as though she'd stepped into an old movie. Nowhere else was the evening set up so perfectly. As the waitress took their wine orders, Mateo offered to order bruschetta, and Peyton jumped on it.

"One of my favorite restaurants in Sacramento is this Italian place," she gushed. "And they do an interesting bruschetta with melted cheese on the top of the bread before the tomato topping. I always inadvertently judge any other bruschetta I eat against that."

Mateo's eyes twinkled at her from across the table. "Well, this is a small-town Italian restaurant. We can hope for the best. But you'll have to let me know how this place measures up. Next time, instead of taking you out, I'll bring you some of my grandmother's tamales. Her tamales are divine."

He said *next time.* A possible second date? Peyton wanted to swoon off her plush chair.

"I've only ever had tamales once," she answered. "And I'll admit, I don't think they were very good. It was off some food cart that the Department of Education had set up for an event." Peyton leaned forward. "And can I tell you something honestly?"

Mateo leaned across the table as if they were in a conspiracy. "Yes, please tell me something honestly."

Peyton giggled under her breath. "I'm not even sure the people who made them had ever made tamales before. I've seen and heard of how amazing tamales are, and these were *not* those tamales."

Mateo burst out in laughter, leaning back and running his hand through his thick hair.

"Fortunately for me, then the competition is really low for my abuela's tamales."

"Well," Peyton answered with her wide smile, "at least it guarantees I'll like your abuela's tamales more than I liked those ones."

Their wine arrived. They had both ordered deep rich reds that appeared burgundy in the dim light. Mateo reached for his fine-stemmed glass, and Peyton admired his frame as he leaned in his chair. She'd thought it was his uniform and his vest that made him appear so broad, but she had been wrong. Mateo had a solid build, packed with muscle across the chest, with thick arms that strained against the fabric of his button-down shirt.

As much as Peyton hated to admit it, she was feeling horny for the guy. It *had* been over a year, after all. If he offered some action tonight, she knew before the appetizer was even on the table that she was going to say yes.

Yes, yes, oh yes.

They barely made it to the car before their hands were on each other.

His kisses were aggressive, forceful, like he knew what he wanted, and he would take it.

But he didn't have to take anything. Peyton wanted to give her all.

She opened her mouth and sucked on his tongue as he pressed her against the cool metal of his car. One of his powerful hands clasped the back of her head, keeping their lips sealed, demanding more of her mouth, of her tongue, of her.

Her arms wrapped around his broad shoulders —his brawn that was purely him — all skin and muscle and Mateo. He ground his groin into her hips, and his other hand ran down her back, curved around her ass and lifted her leg against his. His fingertip traced the length of her outer thigh against the denim, and Peyton moaned into his mouth.

This must have lit him on fire, because his kiss grew more frenzied, and his lips slipped down her chin to her neck and sucked on the tender, yielding skin under her jaw. She dropped her head back to allow him better access. His hand behind her head moved to her neck, cupping it lightly but with an underlying hint of power, of absolute control. Her hands gripped at his shirt, like she was falling, and Mateo was the only solid thing she had to hold on to.

He lifted his lips from her neck, and she shifted her head forward, staring into the ebony whirlpool of his eyes. They shared that gaze as they panted against each other.

"What do you want, Peyton?" he asked in his raspy voice that told her what he wanted. He wanted her on her back or bent over, driving into her. He wanted every inch of her skin. He wanted to find his orgasm with her. But he was giving her the choice. She stared into those eyes that captivated her and lifted her palm to the sharp planes of his cheek.

"You. I want you. Take me somewhere."

He didn't have to be asked twice. His skin burned in a bronze fire as he grabbed her hand and rushed her to the passenger side of his car. He then folded his thickly muscled body gracefully behind the driver's seat and raced to his place. She rested her hand on his thigh and leaned into him as he drove wildly to his apartment.

He grabbed her hand again and rushed her to his door, fumbling with his keys to get her inside. Once the door was open, he didn't stop. He was continuous movement — his arm around her waist, his lips on hers, and once he kicked the door shut, he placed his hands on her ass and lifted her easily to his hips. Peyton wrapped her legs around his waist, clinging to him. Ready for him.

There was nothing else in the world but the two of them, his body and hers, and they would lose themselves in each other.

His hands gripped her thighs hard enough to leave marks, but she didn't care. All she wanted was Mateo, to see if his cock was as thick as the rest of him, and to have him deep inside her, grinding to her core. She craved him. And she wanted him now.

The bedroom was a sight better than what she'd expected from a typical bachelor pad, with a cushioned comforter that she sunk into when he finally released her on the bed. Mateo didn't bother to unbutton his shirt but whipped it over his head.

Peyton's gaze ignited at the sight of his chest. She'd dated and slept with men who were well-built — hell, it was California after all. But this — he was like something from a superhero film. His chest was broad and defined, darkened with a smattering of hair as black as the hair on his head that narrowed down his firm belly to the button of his indigo blue jeans. Just as quickly as her gaze slipped down his body, his hands were unbuttoning his jeans, sending them down his chiseled thighs. Everything about him was thick — his chest, his thighs, his cock that pulsed and throbbed, begging for her touch.

His eyes burned into hers the entire time he undressed. She moved her hands to pull her shirt over her head, but he stopped her. His naked body in all its bronzed glory leaned over her, and she sat up to let him lift her shirt over her head. Mateo placed a knee on the bed between her thighs and cupped her breast in her lacy, buff-colored bra. The stark contrast of her pale skin against his dusky hand caused her to pant harder, as if that contrast made what they were doing in the hazy light of his bedroom real. This wasn't some fantasy she imagined, but a heated moment of reality.

Mateo's own breathing increased as he gazed at her breasts, and his hand moved to the band on her back. With an expert flick of his fingers, the bra released and dropped to her lap. He again cupped the rounded globes, like ripe peaches, and the heat of his hand burned her to her core. Peyton's breath caught as his fingertip brushed against her nipple.

Then he groaned from deep inside his chest, a guttural, animalistic groan, and he whipped her jeans down so quickly she didn't have to lift her hips. She waited for him to tug her lacy panties off as well, but he didn't.

"Spread your legs for me, babe," he whispered.

Her legs moved as if she had no control over her own body, as if she were his to command, and he shifted down between her thighs. Resting his hand at the vee of her legs, he covered the lace with his palm, as if he were claiming her body for his own. His face replaced his hand, and through the sheer lace, his mouth covered her dampened pussy lips, his hot breath mixing with her own heat.

His tongue followed the trail of his mouth, with only the thin fabric of her panties separating her quivering folds from his touch. Through the lace, his tongue moved, going as deep as it could, until it found her clit. The soft pattern of her panties, now hot and wet from his mouth, rubbed against her with alternating pressure from his tongue, hard and fast, then soft and sweeping. She glanced down at him between her thighs, his dark head and muscled shoulders shifting as he claimed her body with his skilled mouth. Peyton pressed her head back and sunk her fingers into Mateo's short hair, clenching at him as he used her own panties to drive her to the brink.

The buzzing between her legs surged through belly to every part of her body, to her fingertips and hair, and she gasped out his name, begging for him. "Mateo."

And he answered immediately. She squealed as his mouth lifted from her clit, and he yanked her panties off her legs. He moved with precision, a man who knew exactly what he wanted and how to claim it. Every capable movement he had in uniform was only accentuated when he was stripped bare with Peyton in his bed.

They had been hushed since they entered his bedroom, with only her begging his name as she came, breaking the quiet. From this point on, they didn't need words — their bodies spoke for them.

Mateo grabbed a silver packet from his bedside table and rolled the rubber over his throbbing cock before he settled his hips against her. The tip of his dick quivered at her opening that wanted him as much as he wanted her. His hand traced her hip to her thigh, lifting her leg against his body as he stared into her eyes.

Again, no words, but he waited, poised, and it took her a minute for her to understand he was waiting for her permission. She nodded, and in a rush he thrust, driving himself inside to the hilt.

With one hand on his shoulder and the other grasping his bedding, she clenched her fingers deep into both, digging fingernail marks into his skin. With leisurely slowness, he pulled back, then thrust again. His pacing was a nightmare, a dream, an impossibly controlled series of movements that rocked Peyton to her core. He shifted slightly and lifted her leg over his shoulder, so he rubbed against her clit again as his thick cock touched every part of her inside, and that roiling buzz built in her again, wiping her consciousness from her as her pussy convulsed around him.

He ground into her, the pace increasing, but his eyes never left hers until he began panting harder, his thighs clenching against her. Peyton slammed her hips against his in return, forcing him to come. Then he squeezed his eyes shut and threw his head back, groaning as he stiffened, before thrusting once more, as if trying to jam his hips even closer to hers.

Instead of collapsing on top of her, he caught himself on his elbows and gasped breathlessly. Peyton cupped the back of his head where his hair was damp from his exertions.

She dropped her leg from his shoulder. Then he lowered his face and kissed her lips, a gentle, inviting kiss that held the promise of more than this one night sharing of bodies.

"I'll have to go home sometime," Peyton told him.

They'd lain in his bed for a while, basking in the glow and the fall back to earth. Now that Peyton's brain was back in her head, it was time to re-enter the real world.

"But not right now," he mumbled into her hair.

Peyton patted his arm. "No, not right now."

"And you'll come back soon?" he asked. She giggled at that. He sounded a bit like a little kid hoping for a treat.

"Maybe my house next time? Then I can make you coffee in the morning."

He lifted his head. "You're offering to let me stay the whole night? Not going to kick me out of bed at three am?"

Her fingers tickled over his arm as she snuggled in deeper.

"No, I could get used to this."

"When?" he asked.

Peyton twisted her head to look up at him. "What? When what?"

"When can I spend the night at your place?" His eyes were closed as she spoke, but his full lips twitched with a smile.

"Why, you got to fit me into your schedule?"

Mateo shook his head, his lips relaxing in that full, amiable smile. "Nope, I just want it to happen as soon as possible."

Peyton nestled into his hard body. She couldn't disagree.

Craving

Chapter Six

THE FOLLOWING WEEK was busy for the both of them, but that coffee appeared on her desk every morning. They were able to meet up for another big date once more before the holiday. This time, they reclined in her bed, their bodies entwined under the fluffy comforter, like a puffy, quilted barrier to the world. Here in bed together, the rest of the world didn't exist — not the problems he'd been having on campus with the vandalism nor the mounds of paperwork she had in regard to this new assignment. Or the larger, looming fact that she was leaving in a few months.

Under the creamy white comforter, there was only the two of them.

Peyton had to admit she was beginning to have concerns about what would happen when she left at the beginning of June. She *liked* Mateo. A *lot*. More than she wanted to admit to herself. But what about Mateo? Did he realize as she did that this relationship was going to be short-lived? That they were on a timer, and that timer was counting down to zero, ready to expire at the end of the semester? So far, neither of them had talked about it, as set as they were on enjoying their time with each other, exploring each other, and discovering each other.

And then moments like this, with Mateo's thick finger exploring every curve and crevice of her skin, she didn't want to think about it. But sometimes her brain did what it often did — trailed off in a cacophony of thoughts. Mateo had spoken to her, and she tried to figure out what he'd said.

"Pardon me, what'd you say?" Peyton tried not to blush every time this happened.

She was unbelievably embarrassed, but Mateo didn't seem to mind. He accepted it easily, as though flighty dates were normal. Who was this guy? How was he the type of person who was handsome, sexy, and didn't hold her distractible nature against her?

The whole package, I think it's called, she said to herself. *That's Mateo.*

"No problem."

Every time her brain checked out, he said *no problem.* How did he *not* find it a problem? Didn't she irritate him? Right now, though, she wasn't going to think about that too much, no matter how much his behavior marveled her. Right now, she planned on concentrating on the question he was asking her. She swept her eyes over his bronzed skin, his clear forehead, his shining eyes that focused on her.

"I was wondering, what you were going to do for Christmas? Are you going home for the holidays?" Mateo asked casually.

"My parents live up near the bay area in San Jose, so I'm leaving Thursday after I'm done with some work and I'm gonna drive straight through."

"Drive straight through? How long of a drive is that?" His clear forehead crinkled a bit.

"It'll take me about eight hours." Peyton answered. "It's not a bad drive though, and the worst will be hitting traffic through LA, but I'm hoping since I'm leaving early on Thursday, I'll get through LA before the traffic builds too much. Once I'm past the Grapevine, everything thins out." Mateo's index finger traced her eyebrows and down the bridge in circles as she spoke, distracting her. As if she weren't distracted enough! "Since Christmas is on a Sunday, I took the Monday and Tuesday after off. My boss kind of owed it to me, of course."

Here she gave him a bit of a side grin. She'd already told him about some of her issues with this assignment — the move alone notwithstanding — and he gave her the same side smile back.

"I'm hoping to be back Monday night," she finished.

Had he wanted to spend Christmas with her? Something in her chest quivered, and she hoped coming back so soon after Christmas would be enough. Mateo sat up over her, his bronze chest glistening like something out of a Greek myth. She ran her hands over the defined planes and the slightly curly hairs between his hard pectorals.

"Will you do me a favor?" he asked, and Peyton shifted from his mesmerizing chest to his face, which was earnest and soft and painted with a look of concern.

"Yeah," she answered. "Yeah, I can do you a favor."

His finger lifted in her entire hand, and he kissed the palm. Her breath caught in her throat at the gesture. "Text me or call me before you leave, then call or text me when you get there. Then call and text me before you leave to come home, and text me when you get home."

His eyes were like shadowy pools, and she was losing herself in that deep gaze. It seemed like a very simple request, but he appeared concerned about her response. She squinted at him.

"Yeah, yes. I can do that. Can I ask why? Is something going on?"

His jaw shifted, and his finger moved to her neck, over her breast, and he caressed her sternum.

"No, nothing's wrong. I wanna make sure that you get there safe and then get home safe. A lot can go wrong in an eight-hour drive, and it'd make me feel better. You'd relieve my worries a bit if I knew you were safe."

Peyton lifted his hand from her chest and pressed it to her cheek.

"Wow, no one's ever asked me that before," she told him in a husky voice.

Mateo stiffened, but his hand didn't leave her skin. "What do you mean? I can't imagine nobody's ever wanted you to call to make sure you got somewhere safe before."

"Yes, they have." His tone had caused a bubble of giggles to flare up inside Peyton, and she bit her lip to stop it. "Not in the same way. My parents have asked me, my brother maybe asked me to call to make sure I got somewhere safe. But that's about it. Not leaving and coming home. And not someone I'm, uh, dating?"

Her tongue tripped over the word, and she had a moment of panic — were they dating? She wasn't seeing anyone else, and she had been taking their dating rather seriously. But she didn't know about him. She'd only assumed.

Mateo's caring expression hardened slightly, and she wondered if she misconstrued what they were doing here. But then his face shifted again, and she could tell it was her answer to his question that made him stiffen. Mateo was visibly concerned that no one had taken that level of care for her before. Her heart melted completely — her insides melted completely, and she realized the import of the question, of his motivation in asking. Even though she'd only known him a few weeks, he cared for her enough to want to know she was safe. He cared enough to ask and risk having her know that maybe his affection for her ran deeper that she realized.

Quite the risk.

And he didn't know she felt the same.

She loved him for his concern. Her blood pulsed in her temples at that awareness of how deep her feelings were, and how problematic that was. How could she love something she was going to leave?

"Well, *I* want to know," he answered. "I need to know if you're okay, that you got home okay. I want to know you're safe."

Instead of answering, she reached her arms around his neck and pulled his face to hers and kissed him with all the emotion that she couldn't put into words.

Craving

Christmas at Abuela's was a tradition that Mateo had known his whole life. The crispy scent of bunuelos welcoming him as he entered the house, the multi-colored lights on the tree blinking in its own celebration (*white lights?* Abuela had scoffed once when he'd asked. *Who wants so boring a Christmas?*) and covered in angel and star ornaments. Presents in green, red, and gold paper tucked under the tree, and hot cocoa with cinnamon. All the trappings of Christmas with Abuela from year to year, unchanging as Abuela herself.

Mateo bent low to kiss her cheek as he entered, a large bag of wrapped gifts in his hands.

"Oh! *Cariño!* Merry Christmas! Come, put your gifts under the tree and have some cocoa!"

"I've been dreaming of your cocoa all night, Abuela." He grinned at her as he set his presents down and accepted a steaming mug.

"More like dreaming of a hot blonde, eh, Mattie?" Damon's voice carried from the bathroom as he opened the door. Mateo rubbed his hand against the mug and blew on it.

"Look who managed to roll out of bed early for once. I guess the offer of free food was enough to get you here."

Abuela smacked Mateo's arm.

"A hot blonde! *Dios mio*! What is all this? You didn't say anything to me!"

Mateo's face grew hot under her ferocious gaze. "It's not like that. We just started dating . . ."

"Yeah, no. I don't think so." Damon smirked as he reached for his own mug of cocoa. "I saw the look on your face when you came to my house last week. You're into her bad."

"Bad?" Abuela screeched. "Why didn't you bring her?"

Mateo clenched his jaw. "She's spending Christmas with her parents. Can we eat breakfast and get our gifts going?

Abuela waved her hand. "Yeah, but we aren't done talking about this, Mattie."

He shrugged and reached around her for his bunuelo and his eggs.

The day passed as Mateo knew it would — gifts, too much good food, and a series of Abuela's favorite Christmas movies. Damon left after the second film, while Mateo stayed until after the third. He was getting ready to leave when Abuela tugged at his sleeve.

"You are smitten, *cariño*. I've never seen you like this. You're going to bring her here so I can meet her, right?"

"Abuela, we only met like three weeks ago." Mateo tried to brush it off, but his grandmother was right. He was more than smitten, but he wasn't about to tell her that.

He didn't need to. Though Mateo prided himself on having a poker face, his grandmother read him like a book.

"Yeah, and I married your grandfather a month after meeting him. There's no accounting for the heart. Now, why don't you bring her here for New Years? We won't do anything big. Damon might not even be here if he throws some big fiesta. You can stop by his place before coming here. Ring in the new year with me and your new love."

"Abuela," he practically whined, and she waved an irritated hand at him.

"No, *cariño*. I'm not asking. Bring her here. I'll invite a few neighbors and your cousin's family. Nothing too big. Before you go running off with this woman."

"What? What does that mean?"

"You told me she doesn't live down here? She's got some big government job in Sacramento?"

Abuela's mind was a steel trap. Mateo clenched his jaw. "Yeah."

"Well, if you're going to be with her, you might end up moving. I want to meet the woman who's going to drag my grandson hundreds of miles from his abuela."

"I think you're taking this way too far. We've only just met. Had a few dates. I'm not moving anywhere."

Abuela patted his cheek and gave him the most condescending smile imaginable.

"I know what I know. Bring her for New Year's."

He kissed her on her cheek in goodbye and headed from home.

The drive was long. Long and miserable, and it had rained which made the latter part of Peyton's trip even more treacherous. California highways were not renowned for their safety during rainstorms. Add to that people who drive like idiots in the rain, and of course she had a hard enough time focusing on the road, not letting her mind wander to the point where she forgot she was driving. *That* would have been a disaster.

It was a sour end to a wonderful holiday with her family. She'd only been in Southern California for a couple of weeks, but her mother had acted like she'd moved halfway across the globe instead of downstate. The upside was it meant her mother had spoiled her rotten. When was the last time she'd slept in until eleven two days in a row?

Her brother Lucas had shown up Saturday afternoon and was up early on Christmas morning — he lived and worked at a rehab center close to her parents in San Jose and got to see them more than she. Lucas didn't get as spoiled, she thought with a grin.

Christmas Eve games followed by cinnamon roll Christmas breakfast, presents (including the obligatory traditional white elephant gift that her mother got this year — a strange educational package on tree planting that made Lucas, the giver, howl). Then a huge turkey dinner with trimmings and four — four! — different types of pie on the counter. Her grandparents and her Uncle Jake had joined them, and by the time she fell into bed on Sunday night, she'd thought she might burst.

When Peyton left Monday morning, she had the idea she wasn't going back up to Northern California to see her family or any friends again before the end of the semester. *That* realization added to her miserableness, and it kept popping into her mind during the drive home. Peyton tried to keep her mind in that good place of Christmas as she fought the downpour to get back to her apartment.

She got home later than she anticipated and tried to bite back her frustrations. She'd hoped to be home by four in the afternoon to relax a little bit and unpack easily. Instead, she got home after six. Still enough time to relax but she felt agitated. At least she had tomorrow off to recoup before going back to Mount Laguna College — something she actually looked forward to.

The faculty at MLC had been amazing for her first few weeks. She'd had a couple meetings with different departments, and on her drive up to her parents, Dr. Anderson had sent her an email, explaining she'd assign Peyton an assistant to help with the paperwork after Peyton had mentioned it at lunch one day. The excitement over an assistant brought a smile to her eyes every time she thought about it. Dr. Anderson had promised Peyton would receive another email later in the week with a list of students to contact once the spring semester started.

Contacts. That reminded her of the one bright and shiny part of her assignment at MLC — Mateo. As she'd promised, she clicked her phone on his number to let him know she was home safe. He picked up on the first ring.

"Were you waiting for my call?" she asked as he said hello. His deep chuckle vibrated from the other end of the phone.

"Maybe," he answered. "Or a text. How was your drive? The rain couldn't have made it easy."

"It wasn't. I white-knuckled it for sure. But I'm home safe, fed and watered the cat, and now I'm in sweats. How was your Christmas?"

"It was great, but my brother Damon didn't keep his mouth shut. He wouldn't stop talking about you to Abuela."

She had to bite back a smirk. "The elusive brother, Damon," Peyton retorted.

"More like the ex-brother, Damon," Mateo said in a slightly irritated voice. "Now I have two things to bring up to you."

Peyton perked up. "Oh, two? What are they?"

"Do you have New Year's plans?"

"No. I don't know many people down here, remember?"

"Well, that's good. Because you'd have to cancel them otherwise. Abuela wants to meet you at a small New Year's party. We can show up late and leave right after midnight, I promise."

Peyton's stomach dropped. "Your grandma wants to meet me?"

"Um, yeah," Mateo sounded surprisingly unsure. She hadn't heard that tone from him before. "I hope that's okay."

Peyton was quiet for a moment, considering. Then it occurred to her, *why not?* There was really nothing to lose. "Sure. If Abuela wants to meet me, I'll be there."

He exhaled into the phone, and she grinned again. Then his tone shifted. "And the second thing. My grandma made some extra tamales and told me I should bring some to you, seeing as you've never had a proper tamale."

Peyton burst out laughing. "Are you kidding me? A *proper* tamale?" She was a bit surprised and excited — *how thoughtful was Mateo's grandmother?*

"Yeah," he answered, "Abuela was outright offended you ate one from a random cart, so I have a sack of them for you. Have you had dinner yet?"

"Actually no, I haven't eaten. I was already late getting home, and I didn't want to delay the drive by stopping for some crappy fast food."

"Well, this might be a little forward of me, and if you're too tired, I understand. The tamales can wait. I'll keep them in my fridge. But if you don't wanna worry about dinner, I can bring them by. And I'll give you a shoulder massage, no strings attached."

Peyton burst into laughter as she glanced down at her sweats. Well, he'd seen her naked, why not in sweats? "Now, if you want strings attached, we can make that happen," she joked.

Mateo answered quickly. "No, seriously. I wanted to make sure that you got home safe, are able to relax, and didn't have to worry about dinner."

She didn't answer right away and bit her lower lip with the sudden rush as thoughts about the timing of this flooding her head. *Why now?* Why now did she have to find a guy, hell — find a man, who was more than anything she ever could've imagined? A man who was the right fit for her? And she was going to have to leave him.

Peyton blinked back the sudden hot tears that burned in her eyes and adjusted her phone against her ear.

"Just be warned, I'll be in ratty sweats when you arrive," she told him.

Mateo again laughed into the phone with his rumbling chuckle.

"Babe," he told her, "you could be wearing nothing but a potato sack and I'd enjoy it."

Chapter Seven

FOR THE FOURTEENTH time that evening, Peyton patted her sparkly black skirt. "Are you sure it's not too much?" she asked again.

Mateo grinned at her, his bright, sultry smile that lit up his entire face. "You look fine. We'll only be at Damon's for a bit, then we'll head to my grandmothers. We can leave right after midnight."

Peyton checked her phone, trying to distract herself from the nervous quivering in her belly. Two hours. His brother's party, then his grandmother's house.

It wasn't meeting Damon or Abuela that unnerved Peyton. Well, it did a bit, but it was more that she worried she wouldn't make a good impression. What if Abuela didn't like her? What if her flightiness got the best of her, and Abuela was insulted by Peyton's lack of attention?

She didn't want to embarrass Mateo.

He reached across the center console of his car and patted her sequined thigh.

"Don't worry. It'll be fine."

Peyton gripped his hand. "I don't want to embarrass you."

Mateo barked out a laugh. "Embarrass me? How could you embarrass me? I'm proud of you! And you look so hot, I want to show you off. Damon doesn't believe me when I tell him I'm dating a hot blonde. I can't wait to show him he's wrong."

Peyton licked her lips. All the saliva in her mouth had dried up during the drive.

"What if I'm not paying attention? You know how I can get."

Mateo flicked his gaze to her, then back to the road as he slowed. They were in the student housing district and must be nearing his brother's house.

"You can get? What does that mean?"

Peyton dropped her head to rest it on the headrest. "Come on, Mateo. You have to have noticed how I don't pay attention. I even warned you about it."

"Woolgathering, I think you called it."

She *had* called it that! How did he remember things that inconsequential?

"Well, it's a bit more than that. Sometimes I just check out. You've seen it. I've done it in front of you. A lot. You don't seem to care or let it bug you. But I know it bugs other people. They've told me to my face."

Mateo pulled the car up to a curb that was filled bumper to bumper with cars. How he managed to tuck the car into the spot, Peyton couldn't guess. Once the car was off, Mateo rested his forearm on the steering wheel and turned to her.

"What do you mean, told you to your face?"

"It bothers people when they think I'm ignoring them. They get pissed. So I try extra hard to focus when I need to, apologize when I can't, and not let it bother me too much. I honestly don't know how it doesn't bug you."

Mateo's eyebrows were high on his head. "Nothing about you bothers me, except maybe that you're going to be leaving in five or so months. That means I have to cram a lot of time with you before you leave. I don't see you as inattentive or ignoring me. I can tell you're thinking. You have a lot going on in your head, and unlike most of these other irritating people on the planet, you don't say anything until you like what you have to say. I appreciate that. I like that you think long and hard about even minor things. I love that about you. And if other people, including my brother, don't like it, then that's on them."

Peyton's heart surged and her eyes watered at his impassioned speech. Had anyone ever told her that her flightiness was a good thing? Not that she could recall.

"And what of your Abuela? What if she doesn't like it?"

Mateo reached for the door handle. "Abuela? Heck, where do you think I learned to appreciate deep thinkers? I learned from the best."

Then he grinned at her again, moved quickly to kiss her cheek, then exited the car and raced to her side to open her door for her.

Peyton could only stare at the handsome, confident man walking around the car. How had she managed to find this guy?

And why did she have to come all the way to Southern California to find him?

Mateo had been right on all counts regarding his brother and grandmother.

Damon's party had been wild — a mix of students and neighborhood friends, and Peyton only sipped the red plastic cup that someone thrust into her hand as soon as she'd entered. It helped take the edge off when Mateo escorted her up to a young man in a black tank top who was nearly a carbon copy of Mateo. Not quite as thick in the arms and with a touch longer hair, but obviously his brother Damon.

"So, you have met a blonde," Damon had teased when Mateo introduced her. Peyton blushed to her roots as Damon shook her hand.

Mateo smacked his brother's upper arm. "I told you."

"Well, thank you for coming, Peyton. There's more liquor in the kitchen, and if you need some fresh air, there's chairs outside on the back patio. Happy New Year!"

Damon had grinned widely at her and moved to shimmy past Mateo, but not before giving his brother two thumbs up. Mateo had ruffled Damon's hair as the fire of Peyton's blush burned even hotter.

They'd stayed for about an hour, and Mateo had waved goodbye to a happily buzzed Damon. Though Peyton should have felt relieved having finished the first part of running the

Mateo family gauntlet, she'd known that the harder test, Abuela, was yet to come. The sips of beer she'd consumed earlier in the night immediately burned off in nervous anticipation.

Abuela lived on the other side of town, not far from the turnoff to horse properties farther east. Her tidy, stucco ranch house sat back from the road, festively decorated for the holidays.

Mateo had pointed at the multi-colored lights. "Abuela keeps them up until almost mid-January. She loves Christmas lights."

"I assume you and your brother get the honor of putting them up and taking them down?"

Mateo nodded. "Yeah. I'm thankful we live in California, so I don't freeze my ass off while standing on a ladder."

There it had been, Mateo's light and easy personality that calmed Peyton's nerves. She took a deep breath as Mateo opened the front door.

Now she stood before the diminutive woman with flashing black eyes, just like Mateo's, and a stiff, no-nonsense back. Her salt-and-pepper hair was pulled back in a loose bun, light tendrils falling into her face, softening the hard exterior Abuela tried to exude.

Then she smiled at Peyton, and Peyton understood why Mateo admired his grandmother so much. That smile, it was like Mateo's smile, overly-welcoming and one that the recipient could readily fall into. Her entire face lit up with that smile and she reached for Peyton. No handshakes for this woman. Abuela was a hugger.

"Peyton! I've heard so much about you! Come in. Eat!"

Abuela kept her hand on Peyton's back as she patted Mateo's face, then led them to the kitchen. A few other people were in the adjoined kitchen-dining area, and Abuela made quick introductions before preparing an enormous plate of food.

"I can't eat all this!" Peyton tried to protest. She glanced at Mateo, whose smile was wider than his grandmother's, a silly, gleeful grin, one that spurred Peyton to smile back.

"Abuela, she doesn't need all that," he tried to protest.

Abuela flapped a tiny hand at her grandson. "Shush. She's too skinny. Eat. And Mateo, get her something to drink. I'll take her to the family room."

Before Peyton could say anything to the contrary, Abuela whisked her to the couch and asked rapid-fire questions in between Peyton's bites of food. Everything from her family to her education to her job — Abuela even asked about her cat!

Mateo came to her side and set a soda can next to her. "Abuela, come on. That's enough."

Abuela narrowed her eyes at him. "I want to make sure she's good enough for my grandson."

"Abuela!" Mateo's own dusky skin pinked at his grandmother's words. Peyton wished for the couch to open up and swallow her whole. Then Abuela winked at her, like they were in on some secret.

"Really, I need to make sure you're good enough for her, Mattie! Look at her! And her job and everything. You should be so lucky to keep her."

If anyone wanted to be swallowed whole, it was Mateo, who reddened even more. Peyton took a long sip of her soda to stop the laugh that threatened to explode out of her. Abuela was a fine woman, and Peyton adored her after only having known her for a few minutes.

Abuela stood up and patted Peyton's shoulder. "Here, Mattie. I'm done torturing you. Sit with your lovely young woman, have fun, and let's ring in the new year."

Then, as quickly as Abuela had brought Peyton into the living room, she bustled back into the kitchen with her other guests.

"I'm so sorry," Mateo started to say, but Peyton held up a hand.

"No, don't. That was fantastically cute. And she was so fast with her questions, I didn't have the chance to be distracted."

Mateo rested his hand on her thigh and leaned in close to her.

"I think you made a great impression on her," he said in a low, husky voice.

"I hope so," Peyton answered back.

Then Mateo leaned the rest of the way to graze his lips across hers, a kiss that tasted salty and sweet and uniquely Mateo.

"Hey!" a voice hollered from the kitchen. Abuela smirked at them from over the counter. "Save it for the new year! Then you can give her a real kiss, Mattie!"

The other guests cheered as Peyton and Mateo ducked their blushing faces.

And when midnight rolled around a few minutes later, he did kiss her, a real kiss full and passionate and full of promise for the new year.

Craving

Peyton had said her goodbyes to Abuela and was in the bathroom when Abuela cornered Mateo. She poked him in his chest with a red-tipped, short-nailed finger.

"Don't mess this up, Mattie. She's an absolute doll. I like her a lot, and she seems good for you."

Mateo shrugged. "Well, I'll hang onto her while I can. She's only here until June."

Abuela grinned at him. "That's six months, *cariño*. A lot can happen in that time."

"Yeah, but what happens in six months?"

Abuela wrapped her arm around his waist to give him a one-armed hug. "Don't think about that. Think about the amazing relationship you can have with her now, while she's here. And if it's meant to happen, you'll figure something out. And Mattie?"

He leaned down closer to Abuela. "Yeah?"

"Don't mess this up. I like her. She's perfect for you. I think this was meant to happen."

Then she kissed his cheek and headed back to the family room.

If only it were that easy, Mateo thought.

Chapter Eight

PEYTON SETTLED IN after the holidays rather easily. Now it was time to dig in and really get started on this assessment she'd been tasked with. Mateo had spent much of his free time over the holiday with her, and Peyton was enjoying his attention far more than she thought prudent. But now that the semester was in full swing, the real world came crashing in on their little bubble.

She was set to begin touring several schools in the Southern California region shortly after the second semester term started in mid-January. President Anderson, however, had promised her an intern, and she contacted Peyton with the intern email the first week of spring semester.

Craving

Evidently Anderson had put out a call to different political science students in the Poli-Sci department, initially selecting students who best met the parameters to be an intern and kicking back any of those who didn't meet the minimum qualifications. What she had put for the minimum qualifications, Peyton had no idea. All she knew was that three student resumes appeared in her email on Friday, the first week of classes. President Anderson was nothing if not efficient.

Of the selection, all the students had great qualifications, but something about the third student caught her eye. The student's name was Jada Harris, and she had an impressive list of volunteer work. Jada seemed willing to sacrifice her free time to help others, which spoke of the kind of person that Peyton might want working with her. After reviewing all three resumes once more to make sure she hadn't missed anything, she decided. Yes, Jada was the winner.

Peyton sent her choice to President Anderson, and she promised Jada would be at Peyton's office sometime on Tuesday. Then she gave Peyton Jada's email, so Peyton could work everything else out with Jada directly. President Anderson said she could only offer her 10 paid hours a week, but Peyton had an idea that would be more than enough for someone like Jada. According to her submitted schedule, Jada had early morning classes, and most of her afternoons were available. Via email, they agreed that she would work for Peyton on Monday, Wednesdays, and Thursdays from 12:30 until 3:30, with a floating hour to do work at home if Peyton needed it. Jada was ecstatic with the schedule, as evidenced by all the capitals in her email,

The young woman who showed up at her office was a bit of a surprise to Peyton, however. Whatever she thought someone who volunteered for a local elementary school looked like, Jada was not it. She was a striking young woman, no doubt, but her bright pink hair and combat boots weren't what Peyton expected at all. But Peyton knew that a person's outside rarely reflected their insides, and Peyton was the first to acknowledge *that* truism. Peyton looked put together on the outside but was a disaster on the inside. She gave Jada credit for pink hair. How awesome just to be herself.

Peyton rose from her chair and extended her hand to Jada as she stepped into Peyton's office.

"You must be Jada. I'm Peyton Clark, and I'm so glad to have you. I need so much help."

Jada gave her a wide smile, warming to Peyton's welcome. Jada shook Peyton's hand with a firm grip for such a tiny pink-haired woman, and she smiled back.

"When this opportunity came up, I made sure I threw everything I had at it," Jada told her in an animated voice.

Peyton stepped back to her desk and perched on the edge, crossing her arms over her chest. That was the kind of eager excitement that reminded Peyton of herself.

"Well, come in and have a seat. I'll kind of explain to you what we do and what you'll be doing for me. We can get you started today. How does that sound?"

Jada scrambled into the chair opposite Peyton and sat with her backpack at her feet. Before Peyton could continue, the young woman grabbed a pad of paper and a flamboyant pink pen from her backpack and sat ready to take notes.

Peyton was already liking her rapport with her first employee. Jada was going to work out well.

"Ok, I'm ready," Jada said.

Craving

You certainly are, Peyton thought as she grabbed her planner off her desk.

The break-ins and vandalism at MLC had increased over the month. Peyton watched as the custodians scrubbed the side of the Learning Resource Center, trying to remove the swaths of black and blue paint. The symbols and words were not legible, but the indelible mark would remain, and the custodians would have to repaint the building to cover the tagging fully.

The recent break-ins were starting to wear on Mateo. Peyton could read it on the lines of his face. He'd also confided in her that his partner was struggling to function and had shown up drunk a couple times, and he was worried about what that would mean for both his partner and for himself.

They cuddled on her couch and watched brain-numbing television. After the hectic holiday and a few brief day trips she'd made to other colleges, they'd spent more time together, enjoying being with each other. And while they sometimes talked campus work, most of their conversations had focused on their lives. And his comment on the increase in break-ins was the first time Mateo mentioned anything that might be a problem. Peyton lifted her head from his arm.

"Is it that bad?" she asked. "Does it mean something?"

"I wouldn't say bad, but definitely an uptick," Mateo answered. "Something we need to keep an eye on and start looking into more. We usually got one or two taggers a semester. Nothing like this."

"Do you have any idea what could be causing it? Or who's behind it?" Peyton asked. "I've been gathering information from a lot of the schools around here, and many of them have noticed an increase in student activities regarding politics and the like. Could it be related to something like that?"

Mateo ran his hand through his hair. "I'm not sure. Have you noticed any trends with an increase in student population leading to an increase in these types of activities?"

Peyton paused at this question. Her work wasn't confidential or anything, but she wasn't exactly making connections like that. So far, all of her inquiries had related to student services and how to best support students. Nothing had indicated a need for increased security or a change in policy regarding negative student activism. That was something she hadn't even begun to consider.

"Why? Have you noticed it with the increase in student population on campus? I don't recall the student attendance numbers offhand." Peyton asked tentatively.

"Hell. I don't know the answer, either," Mateo said. "I don't know what our student population presently sits at, and I don't know the percentages for increases. But it may be something to look into. With any city or town or county, when there's an increase in population, typically there's an increase in criminal activity and police presence as well. Is that something the Department of Education is looking into? Security?"

Peyton tapped her finger on her leg and gazed at Mateo. She was losing herself in him again. Sitting next to her with his hair askew, he looked absolutely dejected. He'd been so high-spirited for her since she'd arrived, she'd never thought he might have problems at work. The weight of what was going on at the campus fell solely on his shoulders, and Peyton hated it. She wanted to do what she could to help fix it. She considered his questions more as she realized that this wasn't just *his* problem as Mateo thought (*well, maybe his drunk partner was his problem*). The uptick in vandalism was a campus-wide issue, a college-wide problem across the state, and it was something that had to be looked at. Maybe better student services could lower those instances?

"Hey, babe," she said, finally slowing down the thoughts racing through her head.

Mateo looked up, his eyes sad and tired. He'd worked considerable overtime as the school tried to clamp down on the break-ins.

"I definitely think it's something that we need to look into," she continued. "Items such as security cameras and key codes might need to be increased on campuses all around California. And student services might help mitigate some of those instances, too. We should look into it. "

A wash of relief touched Mateo. The tension in his neck and his jaw seemed to relax, softening his. He reached his hand over her legs and took her hand in his warm grasp.

"You said *we*," he answered.

Other than the problematic future of her leaving MLC, the first month they'd spent together had been light and fun. This was the first major problem they'd encountered, and it wasn't between them or about her or their relationship as Peyton had expected, given her history. Vandalism on campus was a problem that they could try to solve together.

"I said we," she said before kissing him.

Peyton should have realized that her luck was running out after the conversation with Mateo. The Winters building was hit by the break-ins the next day.

Peyton was fortunate that her office wasn't the focus of the attack. However, two of the windows on the opposite side of the building facing the parking lot were hit. From what Mateo had told her, nothing had been stolen from those offices, but the window damage was pretty extensive, and facilities was going to have quite a time trying to refit new windows into the ugly stone building.

Mateo decided to check in on Peyton and headed to her office. Her office door was mostly closed, so he knocked gently before poking his head in to say hi and update her on the break in.

"Hey, so it looks like it was some kids being stupid again," Mateo confirmed as he stepped into the office. The paraphernalia on his vest jingled as he leaned against the doorframe, and a look of relief washed over Peyton, bringing a touch of pink to her cheeks. It was then he noticed the pink-haired young woman flipping through papers in the far corner of the room. Mateo raised a questioning eyebrow. Peyton waved to hand in Jada's direction.

"This is my new intern I mentioned. Officer Rivera meet Jada Harris," Peyton introduced them. Mateo gave a slight nod to Jada, who returned with a small wave, barely looking up from her work. Mateo turned back to Peyton.

"Your own office *and* an intern. Look who's moving up in the world."

Peyton smiled and reclined into her desk chair. "Not quite." Then her face grew serious. "So what happens with this vandalism thing now?"

Mateo shifted so his broad shoulders filled the doorway. "I'll file paperwork. Check video cameras. Try to follow up. That's about all we can do."

"Do I need to be worried about this? Will something else happen? I have some important documents and computer stuff in here." Her blue eyes widened as she scanned the room.

"I don't think so. The only thing that worries me is your position here is governmental, not academic. It could be some anti-government thing. But since it's been going on for a while and we don't know who's doing this—"

"You mean the windows on campus?" Jada asked from the corner of the room. Peyton rose and stood next to Mateo, who stiffened. Did Jada have an idea of what was going on?

"Do you know something about this? Any information will be useful." He pulled his notebook and pen from the breast pocket of his vest.

Jada tapped her pen against the stack of papers in front of her. "Not much, but you know, in class and stuff. One of the student political groups has been getting a lot of flak for advocating violence. A student in my speech class just left the group. She was complaining that they were too radical for her."

Mateo clicked his pen. "You remember the name of the group? Or the girl who left it?"

"Not the group," Jada said as she shook her pink hair. "But the girl in my speech class is Indigo, like the color? Not sure of her last name."

"That's okay. I can look that up." Mateo tucked this notepad away and faced Peyton. "Thanks for letting me talk to your intern."

"Who knew she'd help you break the case?" Peyton gave him a tight grin and lowered her azure gaze to her desk. "Do you need anything else, Officer?"

Mateo didn't miss the teasing tone of her voice, and her lips curled into a half smile. He had to stop himself from leaning in to kiss her.

"I'll call you later, okay?" he asked, his voice dropping, his gaze intense.

Peyton winked at him. "Of course."

Mateo closed the door as he left her office.

"Dating the campus cop?" Jada piped up from the corner. "Nice."

Peyton pursed her lips. She knew it was probably obvious — there was no hiding their interaction.

"Not quite." She brushed off Jada's curiosity. "Now let's get this paperwork underway before I leave next week."

Craving

Chapter Nine

"I'LL MISS YOU while you're gone," Mateo told her while they laid in bed, between kisses he placed on her neck, between her breasts, and on her belly. He rested his chin right above her belly button and flicked that mesmerizing black gaze to her. Her heart caught in her chest every time he looked at her that way.

"I'll be gone for less than a week. A few colleges down here are close enough where I don't have to stay overnight. The campuses north of L.A, those I can't make as a commute. The traffic alone is outright traumatizing." Peyton ran her hands through his cropped hair. "You sure you're okay feeding my cat?"

"Marmalade seems to like me well enough. We should get on fine."

"Thank you for doing this. I don't know what I would've done. He's okay with a giant bowl of food and water, but that's a long time by himself. You're the only person I feel close enough to ask."

"Close enough?" Mateo asked suggestively, wagging his eyebrows. Then he rose over her, sliding skin against skin. Her knees lifted to wrap around his hips in a familiar movement. "I like being close to you," he whispered.

Peyton threaded her arm around his neck. "And I like it when you're close to me."

Mateo rested on his elbows against her shoulders and cupped her face with his broad hands.

"How close is too close?" he asked, his lips drowning in her hair.

She shifted her head, not sure if she heard him right. What did he mean?

"Is anything too close?" she asked.

"That's what I'm asking. I want to know if I can be too close." His voice rasped against her ear, and her chest suddenly felt heavy, as if the weight of the emotion behind his words sat on her.

"I don't think so. I said, I like you close."

Mateo lifted his head to stare into her eyes. His face was open, honest, his eyes sparkling and intense. Her heart leapt into her throat.

"Because I'm falling in love with you, hard, and I need to know if that's too close."

Peyton had no words. For once, her focus was completely and utterly on the muscled, handsome man in front of her.

When was the last time a guy had expressed any sort of affection for her? Maybe college? Shortly after? And that hadn't been love — that had been temporary lust at best.

But here she had this man, a strong, engaging man who thought about her and her needs even when she didn't. And her mind drifted to him daily. His smile, how his earnest eyes hid behind those reflective sunglasses, how his chest seemed larger than life in uniform and out, the tight curve of his perfectly sculpted ass, the way he laughed at her jokes and was patient with her flightiness.

Oh my god! I'm in love with him!

But could she say such a thing out loud? She didn't have the courage he did. Mateo was the embodiment of courage, at least in Peyton's eyes.

Then again, here he was, that open face putting it all on the line for her when he had no idea where her heart lay. Could she do anything less for him?

Her hand moved of its own volition, cupping the curve of his cheek, his stubble bristling against her palm. His eyes studied hers with such force that tears sprung up under her lashes. How did he manage to gaze into her eyes as if he were looking into the very center of her?

"No," she whispered into the suddenly heady quiet of her bedroom. "Not too close for that at all."

Could she bring herself to say the words? She'd never said them to anyone other than her parents and brother, and those weren't words that marked her heart. This, with Mateo, was shockingly different. This was something from the realm of poetry and heat and intoxication that she'd only seen on TV or in fairy tales. To experience the depth of a man's love like this — a protective love where his focus was on her and her alone?

Craving

Peyton found herself asking, *who does that?*
Mateo, Mateo does that. He does it for me.

She opened her mouth to try to form the words, to share his heartfelt declaration back to him as best she might, but he saved her from herself by capturing her lips with his.

Their kiss shared the language that their voices were unable to put into words.

A week later, Mateo arrived at Peyton's house within moments of her getting home from another campus tour. He'd sent her a text with two words, *I'm here,* and when she opened the door, he didn't ask to come in. He pushed himself at her and cupped the back of her head to force her lips to his. He pressed her back inside the apartment and kissed her like a man desperate for food, desperate for air, desperate for the very core of his own self, and if he didn't kiss her if he didn't touch her, he wouldn't survive.

And Mateo had to wonder, would he survive without her?

No. No, he wouldn't.

He had a brief flash of that awareness as he crushed his body against hers. His tongue delved between her lips, exploring her secrets. Her hands dug into his shoulders, her fingernails raking at him through the thin fabric of his T-shirt. She kissed him back with the same fervor, which only made Mateo moan and grow more aggressive. He growled into her mouth, and before she could respond and without removing his lips, he shifted and bent slightly to scoop her up into his powerful arms. Then as they devoured each other, he rushed into her bedroom and settled her on her bed.

He dragged his mouth to her neck to the open V of her shirt. With deliberate ease he undid the buttons on her shirt one agonizing button at a time, as though he were opening a gift, the greatest, the most precious gift he could have.

Peyton leaned on her elbows and dropped her head back as he finished. Her white lace bra cupped her breasts, offering him her body as if it were that gift. He reached behind her with one hand to release the clasp and lifted it over her breasts, giving him access to her rosebud nipples. He continued his line of kisses down, circling one breast and the other, sending shuddering waves throughout her entire body. His tongue and lips were electric on her skin, and she only wanted more.

He moved to pull away and move lower, but she grabbed him to hold him in place. His cock throbbed at her hip, demanding, and he suckled deeper. His hoarse voice broke the silence.

"I missed you," Mateo said with his lips still against her skin, which was warm and salt-kissed under his mouth and tasted of savory vanilla, and all he wanted to do was go lower and enjoy his meal that was Peyton.

"When you were gone, it was like a piece of me was gone." Her fingers flexed in his hair as he spoke against her skin. "And now that you're back, I'm going to show you how much I missed you."

Peyton sat up so her breasts pressed against his thick chest still covered by his t-shirt. A whisper of a smile graced her face. Her blue eyes burned into him. Her fingers danced along his abdomen to find the hem of his t-shirt, and he bent so she could yank it off his back and over his shoulders.

Her hands then moved to his pants, unfastening the button and zipper and sliding everything down so he stood before her, nothing more than his full bronzed self. Leaning over her on the bed, he pressed another kiss to her lips as his own hands slipped between them. He unfastened her jeans and shifted them and her panties down her thighs and off, so she, too, was as open and exposed as he. He shifted his kisses lower down her neck again, but she grabbed him, holding his head in place. Her gaze bored into his eyes with a longing intensity.

"I hadn't expected it," she whispered to him. "But I was dreadfully lonely when I was gone. I missed you, too. I don't know what it is about you, Mateo, but I can't get enough of you."

Then she pressed her hips to his, and he took her hard and fast, a desperate, shared need between the two of them.

Afterwards, they laid together in bed, her back pressed against his chest as his lips glided over the exposed skin on her shoulder and neck and his hand cupped her breast. The air was still in the bedroom, heavy with the scent of their sweat and musk and their lovemaking — no sound but the two of them breathing together in blissful unison. It seemed to Peyton that they were breathing with each other, or rather *for* each other. When Mateo came to her today, he had an air of impenetrable desperation, of a need that only she could satisfy. And when he moved inside her, their connection was so deep it was like a cord that attached them to each other. Every day closer to the day she had to leave, it seemed that the cord shortened and tightened, and she wondered how she was going to be able to cut that cord and leave when the dreaded time came.

Her fingers danced over his hand as his breathing rumbled in her ear. This moment was so perfect, too perfect, and she wondered how she might experience such perfection, only to have it tainted with the knowledge that it was a fleeting perfection? She couldn't stop these thoughts — they boiled inside her in a storm, a hurricane, and the longer they sat there holding each other, the worse the hurricane became.

Peyton blinked back tears. She wasn't ready to cry in front of him, and she certainly wasn't ready to admit how deep her love for him went, or worse, bring to voice having to leave, moving ten hours north, and maybe never seeing him again. A long-distance relationship was out of the question. Neither of them really had the type of job that might sustain that. And her job wouldn't offer her the opportunity to live in Southern California. When you work for the state, you work at the capital. And Sacramento was way too far from Mount Laguna college. Her eyes watered, and she blinked to push back the tears.

Mateo must've felt a shift in her body as his lips moved over the curve of her neck, and he clutched her more tightly in the broad embrace of his arms.

"Hey," he whispered. "Are you okay?"

No, I'm not, she thought but how could she say such a thing to him? How could she ruin this moment of perfection? They still had almost three months together. Peyton swore to herself in that moment, and all those moments of perfection in

Mateo's arms, that she'd do everything she could to live as much as possible and love Mateo as hard as she could until the very minute she had to leave. He was an amazing man, and he deserved no less. She patted his hand.

"No, I'm fine. I promise," she told him in a husky voice. "I'm just relishing this moment. I've never had something like this, the way we are with each other. Such an intensity. You're a very intense man, Mateo, and all I want is more of you."

It was hard for her to admit. The words were difficult to say — forming them on her lips took conscious effort. But she swore to herself to provide the very best for him and she'd give him that. She'd love him as fiercely as she could. His arms tightened, and it seemed every part of their bodies touched once.

"You are a perfect match for me," Mateo said, his voice husky in her ear. "I crave you. And all I want to do is spend every moment of my life with you."

Their breathing slowed, and Peyton's blood pounded in her heart and brain at his words. She knew he was as attached as she, that the tether on his end was as tightly wrapped around his heart as it was hers. Not every moment of his life, though. They could only spend every moment of the next three months.

I have to make the best of this, she told herself as she nestled deeper into his chest, *and live as passionately with this man as I can for the next three months.*

Chapter Ten

DURING HER NEXT month back on campus, Mateo didn't see Peyton as much as he had hoped. The vandalism and uptick in break-ins at the start of the semester had increased into more volatile crime on campus. The entire staff and faculty were on alert, and Mateo and the rest of the campus police had been working overtime and partnering with the local city police to try to track down what was going on.

Campus police had made a few arrests and turned those offenders over to the local police, as was protocol, but these minor criminals had kept their mouths shut. The only thing they said was they did it for the fun of it.

What the hell kind of answer was that? Mateo was frustrated, and he had to fight not to let those emotions show on

his face when he was around Peyton. But his jaw was sore —
he'd taken to clenching his teeth more while at work as a way to
hide his frustrations.

And no matter how hard Mateo or Aaron had pressed, no
matter how long the city police interviewed them, the kids
denied any claim to a campus or political organization. At one
point, Mateo felt like he was banging his head against the wall.
Aaron dealt with his irritation of course by drinking, but he'd
vowed to Mateo to stop adding whiskey to his coffee when he
was working on campus, and thus far he'd kept that promise. His
dedication to his promise surprised Mateo, who was certain
Aaron was going to start drinking more with the added pressure
on campus. Mateo's threats to send him to rehab must have
permeated his alcohol-addled brain.

Mateo, Aaron, and the other officers increased their
presence on campus, added to their patrol, and spent so much
time walking the buildings and the grounds that Mateo was
certain he'd lost five pounds in the last month. Peyton had
commented on the bags under his eyes last time they'd had
dinner. Her concern for him was painted over her face in a heavy
mask, and she'd spent the entire night reaching out and touching
him as though she were afraid he'd disappear into nothingness.
Mateo didn't blame her. He had to admit he sensed that same
fearful emotion.

The one thing he had managed to be diligent about,
however, was that cup of coffee on her desk every morning, only
now to include Mondays, because lately, the only day he didn't
work was Sundays. He was also spending an extra hour or two a
day on campus for added security, and it all pissed him off. His
time with Peyton was counting down way too fast, and this
vandalism shit had to happen now, taking time away from her?

Worst fucking timing.

One afternoon in March, when the Southern California sun was trying to push past the cloudy gray morning, Mateo sat with Aaron in the security office, which was quiet for once. Mateo hunched over the desk, grateful for the moment of quiet, sniffed his uniform shirt and vest, and crinkled his nose. Working the extra overtime, he didn't have time for laundry like he should, and this shirt wasn't going to last another day. Body spray and cologne only masked so much. Making a mental note to hit the laundry room when he got home, Mateo studied the previous month's incident reports when he noticed something odd.

"Hey, Green," Mateo called to him, "take a look at this."

Aaron came over and looked over Mateo's shoulder at the sheets of paper he had spread out on the table next to a campus map. Mateo cringed when caught a hit of whiskey breath.

God dammit, he thought. Green's promise not to drink on campus had been short-lived. So much for the threat of rehab.

They had other things to focus on right now, so Mateo pushed those thoughts aside. He'd deal with Green later. Right now, he saw a pattern emerging, and he didn't want to lose that focus.

"What's up, brother?" Green asked. Mateo pointed to several black Xs on the campus map and held up an incident report.

"Take a look at this. These X's here are incidences of either break-ins or significant vandalism where a window was broken and the like. Then look over here." Mateo moved his finger to some blue circles drawn on the other spots on the map. "This one here was an incident when someone called in suspicious activity where we went over and investigated. These calls came in at the exact same time as this break-in over here." Mateo moved his finger across the map to one of the X's. "And right here," he tapped his finger in another circle, "was another nuisance call that an officer went on, and this X here was a break-in with a potential theft at the same time."

Aaron squinted his blurry eyes at the map and at the stacks of paper that Mateo lifted as he spoke. Aaron may have been a bit sloshed, but he wasn't a fool. And even a drunk fool could see what was going on. Security was being played to give the vandals time to work. These were coordinated events. Why had it taken them so long to see it?

"Holy shit," Aaron said with another puff of whiskey breath. "It's a fucking ploy. Is there something larger happening on campus? Are they plotting like one of those vigilante groups? That's more than a protest. A larger attack or something? A school shooting? Because that's the old fucking bait-and-switch."

Mateo nodded. "Yeah, and because we've never seen this type of stuff on campus before, we missed it. Seems like it started revving up in November, when we started getting more and more of these tagging and broken windows or minor vandalism calls, and then it amped up to interior office break-ins or office windows and a couple of minor thefts. Most of them occurred at the same time as some dead-ass nuisance call."

Mateo twisted in his vest, which limited how far he could turn in the chair, and leveled his frustrated eyes at Green.

"It's a fucking set up. Whoever this group is, they're planning something, and they're testing our response times. We need to be on alert, Green, and we need to notify local police. We need to tighten security on campus. I don't know who this group is, but they're plotting something. And it's got to be something big."

The light on her office phone blinked bright red when Peyton got to work on Tuesday morning. Her steaming cup of coffee was already in its place, ready for her to sip and wake up, and a warm glow pulsed through her as it always did at the sight of her cup. She smiled. She needed that caffeine hit before she listened to any messages on the phone.

The smooth and sweet Irish cream slipped down her throat, reviving her, and she relished the taste and the thoughts of the sultry, dark-haired man behind it before focusing on work. The calendar on her desk marked the end of March. The students had returned from spring break, and a shock of irritation threaded through her chest.

Peyton had grown to hate that calendar, that parade of days leading to the end of her time here in early June. She had ten weeks left with Mateo, sixty-six days, and she despised watching those days countdown.

Setting the paper coffee cup back on the desk, Peyton tried to shift her attention to her tasks of the day, but her emotions regarding Mateo returned to distract her.

She loved the strong, stoic man whose patience with her was unrivaled. She *loved* him. How did someone abandon what they loved?

But her job in Sacramento was a once in a lifetime, capital city only job. And in ten weeks, she'd pack all her stuff up in her car and head back north.

The unfairness of it all ripped at her heart.

Combing her hands through her blonde bob, Peyton chastised herself. There was enough time to gripe over the unfairness of life once she got home. For now, someone had to work on the reports with all the information she'd collected the previous week. Jada had organized the latest student support numbers, but the spreadsheets wouldn't compile themselves.

The blinking light on the phone, though, needed her attention first. As soon as her laptop was plugged in and on her desk, she lifted the receiver and pressed the button, followed by her inbox code.

"Status quo, bitch."

Peyton started, pulled the receiver from her ear, and stared at the phone.

What?

She hit the replay option and listened again, thinking she must have misheard it. Was it a butt-dial or something? No. The same cussing message in that peculiar grumbling voice. Why had someone left her that message? What status quo? Her job was to create more equitable educational opportunities! If anything, she was helping to disrupt the status quo! What did they, whoever *they* were, think she did here on campus?

Then again, some people hated all things government, and Peyton represented that on MLC's campus. Her mind flicked back to several comments Mateo had made about the angst on campus, that some of the graffiti had anti-college and even anti-government social class sentiments.

Without giving it another thought, Peyton erased the message. She had to get ready for another round of college tours and surveys. This message was nothing.

Just some stupid college kid.

Another round of short college visits meant Peyton was gone the rest of the week. She returned on a Friday, and though she was tired from traveling and surveying so many colleges and universities in a few days, she breathed a sense of relief at being back in her own office. The relative quiet, the familiarity, being back with Mateo, worked to ground her and settle her nerves. Texting and phone calls with Mateo didn't make up for the feeling of his strong arms around her, of waking up next to him in the morning, of those intense eyes crinkling with a smile only for her.

She looked to the corner of her desk, expecting to see a cup of coffee in its space, and a twinge of sadness tore at her heart. The corner was empty. Mateo hadn't known when she was getting back — hell, even she'd been uncertain as to how Friday afternoon traffic was going to treat her, so no steaming coffee sat on her desk.

With a grunt, she slammed her briefcase onto her desk. It was overstuffed with papers, notes, and her laptop, and she really didn't want to carry that weight home for the weekend. The past week had been busy, *killer* busy, and she deserved a weekend to herself, no work, no laptop, no notes. And *a lot* of Mateo. She'd texted him when she left California Coast College a few hours ago, detailing what she wanted to do to him the minute she got back.

She smiled wickedly to herself as she locked her school notes in her desk drawer. Oh, those texts! Sexy and fun and exciting all at once.

The laptop, she decided as she shifted her attention back on work, would still come home — if for nothing else than to check personal emails and maybe do some online shopping — but her attaché case was significantly lighter with only the laptop in it.

Once she felt settled at her desk, she eyed the clunky campus phone. It wasn't quite six, but it was a Friday. Had Mateo decided to work overtime tonight?

Deciding to skip the campus phone, she grabbed her cell phone from her purse and pulled up Mateo's information. Maybe she could see him tonight. The thought of it made her thighs weak.

Hey babe. Just got back. Are you home yet?
Not yet. Still on campus. Leaving in a minute. Can I swing by? he texted back.

She tapped at her teeth with a fingernail. Maybe they could drive to her place together. Or go out right now, before she went home. She looked like hell, dressed in a baggy light sweater and her blonde bob hanging in limp strands against her face — she needed a trim, badly — but the urge to see Mateo overrode it all.

I'm on campus. Want to meet up somewhere?

Not even a second passed before the next text from Mateo.

Stay there.

Within minutes, Mateo stepped easily into her office, and she rose to meet him, intending to hug him. He looked so commanding in his uniform that her body throbbed in response to him, desperate to touch him, to press against his hardened body. She paused in reaching for him, however, when he pulled his sunglasses off his face and stared at her with a hard, almost ferocious expression.

"Is Jada here?" he asked, his voice raspy.

Peyton shook her head. "No, she's not here —"

She didn't get the chance to finish before Mateo kicked the metal door shut and crushed his lips to hers.

And she followed his lead. Everything in their relationship had grown more heightened, more intense, and this moment seemed to be the culmination of all that pent up need and desire left unchecked over the past week.

Mateo tore his lips from her long enough to lock the doorknob. Then he turned back to her, one sleek black eyebrow raised in question. Peyton nodded her head, ready for whatever Mateo had in mind.

He moved in a flash, returning to assault her lips as his hands fell to her breasts and hips, grabbing and kneading as if to prove to himself that she was here, in his arms, again.

"Don't leave me again," his gruff voice commanded as he ground against her teeth.

Then he spun her around and bent her over her desk as he ran his hand down the length of her back to the curve of her ass. Chills covered her skin at his touch, at his aggression, at the pure raw nature of his need.

Peyton moved her hand to the front of her linen pants, unfastening the waistband so he could yank them over the round curves of her backside. His breathing was ragged above her as he ran a finger over the lacy edge of her panties. With one finger, he pulled those down to her thighs to join her pants.

She heard the low clanging sound of a belt as he loosened his own uniform pants and the tearing of a condom packet. The smooth warmth of his cock rubbed over the pale globes of her ass before diving low between her thighs, reaching for her wet sheath that begged to be filled. To be filled by Mateo.

Then he was deep inside her, pulsing and pushing. He fell over her, catching himself with the flat of his hand slamming on her desk as he grunted, trying to press deeper. The desktop was cool against Peyton's heated cheek as her body jerked against the surface with every thrust of Mateo's hips.

His cock rubbed against the walls of her love canal, hitting the right spot to make her gasp and arch up on the desk. Mateo pressed her back down as his hips worked faster, ramming into her harder, until his own breathing became panting and raspy, a series of low groans and mumbles.

"You're mine. You're mine," he chanted.

Peyton's panting matched his as her own ecstasy unfurled from her abused pussy throughout her body in a tingling explosion. As she inhaled another squealing gasp, Mateo went rigid behind her, roaring from deep in his chest as he twitched against her thigh, coming hard over and over.

Then he was gone, cool air caressing her hot skin. Peyton pushed herself off the desk and rotated, slowly pulling up her panties and pants over the wetness Mateo left behind. Mateo palmed the used condom and re-fastened his own pants. Peyton grabbed a tissue from the box on her desk, used it to wrap the used condom, and tossed it in her trash can.

A relaxed smile crossed his face as Mateo brushed a lock of fair hair from her forehead before cupping her face and kissing her lightly. A light, loving kiss so contrary to the rough, raw sex they'd just had on her desk.

"I missed you. I couldn't wait," he whispered against her lips.

Peyton placed her palms on either side of his angled jaw.

"I'm back. I'm here," she told him in a silky voice.

They kissed again, avoiding the question that hung heavily in the air.

For how long?

Craving

Chapter Eleven

AFTER HIS SHIFT on Saturday, Mateo spent most of his weekend with her. If absence made the heart grow fonder, it definitely made the cock firmer, that was for sure.

But as most days in spring had done, the weekend passed quickly, too quickly for Mateo and Peyton. Mateo walked her to her car on Monday morning before she left for campus. He finally took a day off and needed to catch up on his own stuff at home, having not been there all weekend.

Their relationship was so easy that Mateo marveled at it. When had any relationship he'd been in flowed like it was supposed to happen? Too many overly dramatic women, too many expectations from him . . . But none of this with Peyton.

Maybe the deadline on Peyton's time at Mount Laguna helped eliminate much of that drama. Mateo didn't know.

What he did know, what he finally had to admit as he threw his uniform into the ancient washing machine, was that he didn't want that deadline to come. He had tried to ignore it, tell himself that he'd deal with the deadline when it came, but none of that was working anymore. Her departure in a few weeks had become an elephant in the room — one that they couldn't ignore any longer. Mateo had realized that he could see himself living with Peyton, having a family with her, growing old with her. All her idiosyncrasies only made him love her more.

He'd never had those thoughts about a woman before.

How in the hell could he make all that happen, that future he'd realized he craved, when she was leaving soon and moving back up to Northern California, over four hundred miles away? Every time he thought about it, a sinking pain curdled in his stomach.

Tell her, he said to himself. They couldn't begin to figure it out or make plans otherwise. *You have to tell her.*

I will, he vowed. *Soon.*

Green sat in the office with Mateo when the call came in. It seemed to be another nuisance call, and it was coming from the athletic field. Mateo flicked his eyes to the campus map they'd been using to evaluate some of the crimes, and he noted the learning resource center was probably the building most directly across campus.

"Green!" Mateo shouted as he rushed to the security office door. "You go around to the learning resource center while I hit the athletic fields. If this is another one of those gigs where they distract us so they can vandalize another building, this is our chance to put a stop to at least this incident."

Mateo clicked on his radio, hearing it squawk as he ran for the far side of campus and the athletic office where a nuisance call had come in. He was almost at the building when he radioed Green. "Green, you copy? Are you at the LRC? What do you see?"

Nothing but dead air on his radio. *Fuck*, Mateo thought. He approached the offices where the main door to the athletic building hung wide open as it should for four in the afternoon. Mateo peeked in, uncertain as to who he'd find. To his surprise, Coach Garcia sat behind his desk with a stack of papers in front of him and an aggravated expression on his face.

"Coach Garcia," Mateo announced as he entered the spartan office. The coach didn't appear to be one for collectibles. Or if he did, he certainly didn't keep him here on campus. And that was probably smart, given the current break-in situation.

The coach's head snapped up. "Hey, Officer Rivera," the coach said in a distracted voice. "I'm sorry. I'm knee-deep in these athletic scholarship forms. You'd think it would all be on the computer by now, but they need wet signatures on these forms."

"So that's all you've been doing this afternoon? You didn't make a call to security?" Mateo asked.

Coach Garcia squinted his eyes at Mateo. "Nope. Nobody here but me and my paperwork. Why, is something going on? Did you get a call from this office?"

"Not quite," Mateo told him. "We've been getting a lot of vandalism nuisance calls on campus lately. We think it might have something to do with some of the protest and riot groups that are gaining traction, using college students to promote their agendas on campus. Most of the calls have been nonviolent vandalism or breaking and entering calls, nothing more serious than that."

"And you got a call from here?" Garcia was suddenly very interested. Mateo didn't blame him. Coach Garcia was renowned for his protectiveness over his athletes.

Mateo clutched at the side of his weighty vest. "We seem to be getting nuisance calls and then vandalism or break-ins will occur elsewhere on campus. It seems to be coordinated, and we're working with local police. If you could help keep an eye out for anything suspicious, or if any of your players mention anything, please let me know. It's not serious yet, but it's starting to escalate."

Garcia nodded and half-rose from his chair. He reached out his hand to Officer Rivera and shook his hand. "Thanks for keeping an eye on the campus and protecting the students and staff. I'll keep an eye on my students and athletes and let you know if I hear anything," Coach Garcia promised.

Mateo tipped his head to the coach as he left, but not before leaving his card with his cell phone number on the corner of Coach Garcia's desk.

As he exited the athletic office, he tried his radio again. "Green! Green, do you copy?" Nothing but a squawk of the radio and dead air. No response.

Fuck, he thought again as he jogged across campus to the Learning Resource Center. Maybe Green was involved with something and couldn't respond. Mateo gave him the benefit of the doubt, even if, deep in his chest, he knew it wasn't true.

The LRC was empty, nothing but the building and the broken window at the bottom floor bathroom. Mateo shook his head and clenched his jaw. His anger and fury at Green burned under his skin, popping in sizzling like hot oil in a pan. Mateo nudged the broken glass with his toe and realized that if they didn't get a handle on Green's drinking, or his general lack of enthusiasm for the job, something serious could happen. What if a student had been here? Or in the bathroom? What if this all escalated to physical violence?

Mateo would *not* allow that to happen.

He yanked out his walkie-talkie from its shoulder clip and radioed to facilities, telling them about the broken glass outside the bathroom of the Learning Resource Center that needed attendance. Then he studied the area, searching for anything that might give an indication as to who, or maybe *why,* someone would try to break the bathroom window at the LRC.

He walked around the building, looking for anyone who might be loitering unnecessarily, and then went inside to see if someone had thrown a rock into the restroom or something like that. Nothing inside but more broken glass. Mateo reached into his vest to pull out a narrow roll of caution tape and crisscrossed it over the broken glass area. He then radioed facilities again, informing them there was also glass inside the bathroom

In a huff, Mateo exited the bathroom and stood in the tiled lobby of the LRC. The library wasn't very busy as it was getting close to dinner time. Most students were either leaving class, going home, or heading out to work. They were going to grab dinner, not necessarily go to the library. However, a few students milled about, coming in and out of the building, so he approached them and began questioning with his standard line of inquiries.

Did you see anyone on campus who maybe shouldn't be here?

Did you see anyone on campus hanging around the men's bathroom in the library?

Did you hear anything questionable?

Have you heard anything about vandalism or break-ins?

And as he expected, all he got were a bunch of blank faces and *I don't know* responses.

Fuck, Mateo said to himself again. Not only were the broken windows and busted locks an added expense to the campus, it didn't exactly look good on Mateo if this kind of stuff happened and he wasn't able to get a handle on it. And obviously Green wasn't gonna be a damn bit of help. No more rehab threats. This time, he was going to follow up. Green had become a liability to the campus. Mateo pressed the radio for Green again.

"Green, do you copy?"

This time his radio squawked, and Green's voice sounded from the tinny speaker. "Yeah, brother. What do you need?"

Mateo blew out his anger in one long breath. The radio was not the place to get on Green's case for a lack of responsibility.

"Where are you?" Mateo barked into the radio.

"I'm at the security office. Where else would I be?"

Mateo rubbed his fingers against his forehead. "Stay there. Don't move. I'm on my way." Mateo broke into a run to get to the security office as fast as he could. The last thing he needed was for Aaron to bail on him, try to hide any whiskey breath he might have. Fortunately, only Green was in the office when Mateo burst through like a bull in a china shop.

"Green, what the fuck is wrong with you?" Mateo hollered, his fury finally taking over.

Green bore a look of absolute vacancy on his face, like he had no idea where he was or what he was doing.

FUCK, Mateo screamed in his mind.

"What do you mean? I've been here the whole time."

"The whole time? I told you to go to the LRC to check on it in case this was another one of those tag-team calls. Why the fuck are you still here in the office?" Mateo's voice was sharp and biting, even though he tried to temper it. Having an anger problem was not a good trait in a peace officer, and Mateo prided himself and his levelheadedness. To lose it now with another security officer who might be inebriated and incapable wouldn't do anyone any good.

"What do you mean, go over there? I was waiting here for the call from the LRC to see if they reported any vandalism," Green answered.

Mateo slapped his hand against his face, a literal facepalm, and he couldn't believe he'd become a joke or a meme because of Green's perpetual ineptitude.

"You dumb ass," Mateo bit out as he walked closer to Green to get right in his face. He was barely an inch taller than the guy, but between his anger and his frustration and his sense of superiority, Mateo felt three times larger than this pathetic excuse for a security officer. "I didn't tell you to wait for the call from the Learning Resource Center. That isn't how this operates. You needed to go there. I said *go* to the LRC." Every time Mateo said the word *go*, he poked Green in his vest, punctuating the words. Green exhaled and sure enough, a wisp of alcohol floated past Mateo's nose.

"Oh," Green said in a sheepish tone. "I thought you meant wait here for them to call and then go to the Learning Resource Center."

Mateo's jaw clenched so hard that he worried his teeth would crack. He took a deep breath, trying to calm his inner anger at this pathetic excuse of a man.

"Let me tell you how this is going to work, Green," Mateo told him, not bothering to hide the rough edge in his voice. "You need to get some help. Now. No more promises, no more delays. Today. We have something serious developing here on campus, and we need security officers who are capable and functional. Right now, you're neither of those. So you need to figure out a way to get yourself cleaned up, today, otherwise I'll be making a few phone calls, and you'll find yourself without a job and in some nasty ass rehab before you can blink."

Aaron backed up from Mateo as though Mateo's words were a whip that stung his skin until he bumped against the file cabinet. *At least he's taking my words seriously*, Mateo said to himself. Green held up his hands in front of his vest.

"Ok. Ok. I've got a lot going on, and I haven't been dealing with it well. So I've been taking a nip with my coffee, a little sip at lunch, and then when I get off duty. But we've had to work overtime, and sometimes that sip at night comes before I'm off duty. But I'll get it under control. I'll stop drinking on the job. Please Mateo. Please, brother. I can't lose my job."

Aaron's voice was unbearably pathetic; he exuded a sense of desperation and defenselessness. Despite himself, Mateo was moved towards leniency. Who hadn't been in a bad place and needed a little bit of alcohol therapy to get through it? He just needed Green not to do it on the job.

"You can be as drunk as you need to be at night when you go home," Mateo told him, his finger pointing at Green again. "You carry a weapon. Multiple weapons. You have an obligation. And you need to be stone cold sober when you're here on campus engaging with the students and the faculty and the staff. If I see anything that hints that you've been drinking, a slip up, a slurred word, anything, your ass is mine and I'll report you. No more warnings, nothing. Today is the last day. Do I make myself clear?"

Aaron nodded pathetically. He was like a week-old child, and Mateo had to stop the rising surge of disgust that filled him.

This would be Aaron's second chance. Mateo's mind went to the baseball coach he'd spoken to earlier. Like Coach Garcia always said, *Three strikes and you're out.*

Mateo prayed that nobody would get hurt if and when that third strike came.

The best part of spring, in Peyton's opinion, was the longer days. She loved being able to leave her office and still enjoy the brilliant, multi-hued beauty of sunset. Jada had scrambled to leave as she was meeting up with some friends, and Jada's glee was infectious. Peyton wanted to enjoy the outdoors and even started eating dinner on her small apartment patio on a cheap folding lawn chair. It was the simple things that delighted her.

She'd been running late that morning, which meant her car was parked at the far end of the faculty parking lot. Still closer than the student lot, but with her heavy computer bag and her files she wanted to work on at home, the walk was longer than she cared for, even in the pastel late afternoon sunlight.

Then she had to fumble for her keys. Why hadn't she gotten them out of her purse *before* she'd collected everything in her arms? Resting the files and her laptop bag on top of her car as she reached for her purse, her fingers had brushed against her key fob when a voice called out behind her.

"Hey, lady!"

Peyton swiveled her head back and forth. *Are they asking for me?*

"Hey, lady!" the voice yelled again.

This time she turned around to search for the owner of the voice when a man with a black bandanna wrapped around the bottom of his face rushed up to her.

"You fascist pig! You government drone!" he cursed at her, then he upturned his water bottle and dumped it over her head and ran off.

She didn't have time to react — she barely had time to be scared. Her heart pounded in her chest from surprise tinged with fear, but when she looked up again, the kid was gone.

At least, she assumed it was a college kid. Who else would be protesting her on campus?

Why was he protesting her?

Using the bottom of her shirt to wipe her face, she tried to figure out what was going on. How did this kid know who she was or that she worked for the government? It wasn't like she advertised. And when she was on campus, she was in her office most of the time. And she wasn't some FBI agent — she worked for the Department of Education for chrissake! Government drone?

What was going on?

Her hands shook with unease and frustration as she turned to her car and finished unlocking it. As she put her belongings in her car, Peyton realized she should probably report this to Mateo. And the odd phone call she'd received the week before. He'd been dealing with some strange happenings on campus. What if this kid and his water bottle were part of that?

She palmed her keys and dug in her purse again, this time for her phone. She extracted it and hit the button for Mateo. He answered right away.

"Hello, beautiful," he said in the low, sultry voice she'd come to expect whenever he answered. Even with her wet hair dripping in her face, she warmed at the sound of his voice.

"Hey. So, no big deal, but are you still at work? Something happened, and I think I need to report it."

"Where are you?" His tone shifted, and he was serious, focused. That shift caused a flutter of nerves in her chest that rivaled her interaction with the would-be protester.

"I'm in staff parking C. The far end —"

"On my way."

It wasn't the best time, but she loved how sexy his sense of immediacy was. It exuded a sense of power, and right now, she really needed that.

Not even a minute later, Mateo was striding across the asphalt, the last rays of the setting sun reflecting off his mirrored sunglasses. He lifted them to his forehead as he approached.

Mateo's normally kind and open face was different —
terse and alert. This wasn't Mateo, her boyfriend. This was
Officer Rivera, and he wasn't messing around. His eyes coursed
over her, from her damp head to her feet.

"What happened? Are you okay?" he rushed to embrace
her, crushing her against the firmness of his bullet-proof vest
under his uniform.

Peyton pressed a hand against his chest, pushing slightly
away. "I'm fine. Just wet. This guy —"

"What guy?"

She glanced across the parking lot in the direction she
thought the guy had run away in. "He wore a bandanna on his
face, so I didn't get to see him. Black clothes, pretty basic. He
called me fascist and a government drone and dumped water on
my head."

Mateo's hand cupped her hair, as if touching it made it
real. "Are you sure you're okay?"

She nodded. "Yeah, but there's more, I think."

"More?"

"I got a phone call like a week or so ago. I didn't think
anything of it, a stupid prank, but maybe . . ."

"A phone call? What did the message say?"

Peyton hesitated. "Something about status quo? I can't
recall. I deleted it."

Mateo's face fell at her words.

"I'm sorry. Did I do something wrong?"

His arms tightened around her. "No, nothing wrong. But
I think I need to have a meeting with the other officers and the
admin. And the local police. The threats against you, the
vandalism, the graffiti, something bigger is definitely going on.

Maybe it's more than student protesters. Extremist groups often come to campuses to recruit impressionable students."

"If not students, then who?"

"Anti-government terrorists. They might be using students. This might be a bit bigger than the campus."

Peyton wiped her damp hair off her eyes. "Well, whatever it is, I think the guy today was misguided. I'm a low-level Department of Ed worker. Not a senator or anything. And it's not like I told anyone what I do. What does bugging me accomplish?"

Mateo shook his head. "It's not that easy. To them, you work for the government, that's all they need to know. And word gets around. They might see you as a representative of the government they hate, and here you are, right on their campus. I worry that if they turn really violent, they might take it out on you. The LRC is right across from your building. What if they try to attack your office next? There was already that broken window."

"You don't think that would happen? I don't have anything in there worth stealing, really. Just my notes and some files. Most of what I need is on my laptop or on the Department of Ed server already."

"They might not know that," Mateo answered. "But I'm going to set up a meeting, just in case. I'll start making calls tonight." He looked from her to her car. "Are you okay to drive home?"

"Yeah. But maybe you can swing by after work?"

"Definitely," he said as he glanced at his watch. "In fact, I'm almost off now. Let me shoot an email to the president's office and the other officers, and I'll head out. Sound good?"

She nodded, and he kissed her cheek. Not too much for campus, but it wasn't as if the entire staff didn't already know they were dating. And even now, after this strange event here in the fading light of day, the touch of his full lips on her skin sent a comforting, heated shiver down her spine.

"See you in a bit," she told him, then ducked into her car with her files and bag, closed the door, and drove out of the parking lot.

When she looked in the rear-view mirror, Mateo stood there, watching to make sure she made it out alright.

"We've got a problem," Mateo announced to Green and evening officer Randall Cortes as he sat at the computer to write his email. One of the Mount Laguna City cops, MLC's city liaison Officer Crimson was en route, but not in the office yet. The others could fill him in.

"What now? Another vandalism call?" Green asked.

Mateo shook his head as he focused his eyes on Green. Aaron had been good on his promise to keep his drinking off the job for the past few days, at least as far as Mateo could tell. No coffee-whiskey breath, no wavering voice. He'd been a good boy ever since Mateo unloaded on him. But long term . . . Mateo doubted it would stay that way. It never did.

"No. Peyton was assaulted in the parking lot."

Green half stood from his seat. Cortes rose completely, his face a mask of shock.

"What?" Randall asked.

"Well, not like that," Mateo tried to clarify. "She was approached by a random guy who screamed some anti-government crap at her, then dumped water over her head."

Green's face screwed up as he resettled back into his seat. "I'm sorry, water?"

"Yeah, so no big deal and she's fine. But she also had an anti-government prank call last week, and with the stuff happening on campus, I'm wondering if this is larger than a campus student protest."

"Student protesters usually don't attack strangers. They hold signs and sit in the quad. Why pick Peyton as their focus?" Randall asked.

Mateo shrugged. "I'm only guessing, but if this is more of a terrorist group, and she works directly for the government . . ."

"That might be a stretch. But the campus isn't locked down like government buildings are. No metal detectors or anything," Aaron pointed out.

Mateo aimed a finger at Green. "Right. Easy target. I won't have Peyton be an easy target. I'm sending an email to the president's office, and I've already contacted Crimson at Laguna PD. We need to heighten security, and nothing gets past us. No strange, unpermitted cars, no one on campus who shouldn't be here, keep records of all phone calls. We're on high alert until we figure this out or the ringleaders are arrested. Got it?"

Both Green and Cortes nodded in agreement. Mateo then swiveled in his chair to his computer and opened his email.

It wasn't *that* big of a deal, Mateo tried to tell himself. A prank call and water — nothing too serious. Just some college kids mixed up with the wrong people.

But as he composed his email, a chill swept across his back. A lot of bad things had happened in history when kids got mixed up with dangerous criminals. History was bathed in the outcome of those mix ups.

And nothing, absolutely *nothing*, would happen to Peyton, not if Mateo had any say in the matter.

Chapter Twelve

HE ENDED UP spending the night — something that had become regular when Peyton wasn't out of town. When she was in bed with Mateo, all the stress of her job, her move, everything in the world fell away outside of his embrace. She slept the entire night with his strong, protective arms holding her.

In the morning, they had to drive separately to campus because Peyton planned on leaving earlier than Mateo. He'd already put in for overtime; the weather app on his phone predicted unseasonably high temperatures, and they were nearing the end of the semester. If Mateo knew one thing, he knew that was a recipe for danger, especially in policing.

They parked next to each other near the security office, and as Peyton pulled her bag and files from her car, Mateo raced into the security office and started up the coffee pot with Peyton's coffee, this time hazelnut cream. As it percolated, he ran back out and lifted the stack of papers from her arms.

"Do you need me to take the bag, too?" he asked. Peyton giggled.

"Honestly Mateo, you make me feel like I'm in high school again," she joked. "I don't remember anyone helping me with my books and papers back then."

She smiled widely at him, and the pull of her pink lips and the shine of her sky-blue eyes made his heart melt. How can anyone *not* want to help her carry her books? She brushed her wind-blown hair from her face as she adjusted her bag on her shoulder.

"Okay, I'm ready to go," she told him.

He extended his arm out to let her lead. "Your coffee awaits, milady," he said in a comically formal tone.

"You are too much," she said as she started to brush past him toward campus. Before she could move beyond his arm, he grabbed her around the waist and spun her into the firmness of his uniform vest.

"Never too much for you," he told her in a light voice.

Then he popped a quick kiss on her lips and released her, his eyes swiveling around the parking lot to make sure they hadn't been caught. It was still early in the day, and most of the campus knew they had something going on. Yet, he didn't really want to suffer any teasing or make problems with human resources. Nor did he want anyone to say anything directly to Peyton. She was here on borrowed time. She didn't need any extra drama to go along with this assignment. Instead of giggling this time, her lips closed into a sultry rosebud curl and her eyes narrowed. She gave him a side-long glance as she walked past him. Mateo's chest clenched. If they hadn't had to be at work, he would've pushed Peyton back into the car and taken her right there in the parking lot.

She headed towards the security office door, and he caught up with her to open it. The rich scent of the hazelnut cream welcomed them, and Peyton smiled lightly and Mateo once again.

"Let me get that for you," he told her as he moved past the counter to the coffee pot.

He didn't see hide or hair of Aaron — late again. Or sleeping off a bender? In the john? Who knew at this point?

Mateo poured her a paper cup and grabbed a few sugars and creamers before walking her back outside towards the Winters building. The building's main door was already unlocked. Mateo had a flare of surprise when the door opened easily. Facilities had started to get in the habit of keeping things more locked up for security reasons against the break-ins. But with his hands full, Mateo was grateful that facilities was actually on the ball this morning.

Students milled about in the bright early morning — some rushing for classes, others waving hello to them. It was almost as though he was on a movie set for a college film, that's how perfect the campus seemed. Peyton walked in front of him as they moved down the hall and then stopped directly in front of her door so abruptly Mateo nearly knocked into her. He adjusted her stack of papers and coffee cup in his hand, reaching out his other hand to place it on her waist.

"Hey baby, everything okay?"

Peyton didn't answer right away and pointed with her index finger as the rest of her hand held the coffee cup in her slender grip.

"A package," she said.

The tone of surprise in her voice raised the hairs at the back of Mateo's neck. And that was a sensation Mateo didn't ignore. The main door had already been unlocked, and here was this square, cardboard box she hadn't expected. His grip on Peyton's waist tightened, and he pulled her back into him. He scanned the other offices, looking for an open door or an open window or, more likely, a broken window. The hairs on Mateo's neck rose higher.

"Mateo, let me grab it and head into my office," Peyton told him, tugging away.

He clenched her harder, slamming her against his vest. He set the papers and cup on the ground, then pressed his radio button. "Green."

Nothing but dead air.

Fuck. Mateo thought. *Where the hell is Green?*

Green should've been in the office already, and if anyone had called a delivery into facilities, they would have had to call the security office. Facilities rarely answered the phone, and when they did, they usually didn't open until eight. What worried Mateo more was that someone might have reported a nuisance call somewhere else on campus and left the package here. That was a problem. He might have been overreacting, but a tight sensation in his gut told him he wasn't. He keyed the radio again.

"Green, do you copy?"

Still nothing but dead air. *Fuck.* This time he said it loud enough for Peyton to hear. She twisted her head, her eyes scrunched together as she looked over her shoulder at him.

"What's going on, Mateo? Let me get the box and we'll go into my office."

She lunged forward, and Mateo had a moment of panic as her fingertips brushed the edge of the cardboard. This time Mateo whirled around so his body was a shield between her and the rest of the hallway. Before she could utter another word, he shoved her, nearly throwing her back down the hall toward the main door. Her coffee spilled from her cup onto the floor, and she stumbled as Mateo backed up, his body a barrier between her and the simple square box sitting in front of her office door.

"Mateo, what?"

Mateo put his hand on his waistband and held the butt of his service weapon. With his left hand, he keyed the radio once more. "Green!" *Goddamnit, answer your radio!*

Nothing but static and dead air. Mateo pulled out his cell phone and twisted his head over his shoulder to Peyton.

"Peyton, darling," he said in a constricted voice, "I need you to exit the building now. I'm going to do a search of the rest of the building and get anybody else out of here. Make your way to the security office and tell anyone heading toward the Winters building to leave the area." As he spoke, he pressed the buttons on his phone.

Peyton stood up straight behind him. "Mateo, I don't understand."

"Peyton, listen to me. Get out *now*."

He inhaled to make his body as large as it could be, trying to block as much of the hallway from her as possible. If anything happened, he needed to cover her in an instant. An exhaled breath parted his lips as he watched her from the corner of his eye.

Peyton gathered her bag and slowly walked backwards out the main door. He was grateful that her confused expression became a little more than a blur in his vision. When she was at the main door, the phone finally picked up on the other end at the offices of the Mount Laguna city police.

"Mount Laguna police. This is Officer Crimson."

"Crimson, this is Riviera at MLC. I need you to call the bomb squad. I think we have a bomb."

At Mateo's words, Peyton's blood exploded in a burst of cold throughout her entire body. She stood at the main door to the building, the bar for the metal door hitting her hips.

A bomb? There's a bomb?

And Mateo wasn't leaving with her?

"Mateo, no," she called out in a wavering voice as she pressed against the bar to open the door. "Come on. Wait for the bomb squad."

Mateo turned and quickly approached her, focused determination in the hard lines of his face. At first, her chest lightened, thinking Mateo was going to listen to her and leave. Then his strong arm thrust the door wide, she spilled onto the cement walkway outside the building, her bag and coffee cup spilling around her.

Peyton watched in horror as Mateo's eyes caught hers with black intensity. He mouthed "I love you" before slamming the door closed on her.

"Wait!" she screamed, but Mateo was gone from the door, off risking his life as he searched the building to make sure it was empty.

From her side view, a student ran behind her, rushing for class, and thankfully away from the danger hidden in the bowels of the Winters Building. In the distance, sirens echoed in the early morning, while several students had made their way to the door. Peyton leapt at them.

"No! Come away. There's a bomb threat!"

The students paled and scrambled backwards toward the grassy quad.

Peyton inhaled, realizing what she needed to do. No other campus police had neared the building, which struck Peyton as odd and strengthened her decision.

"Back away!" she called out as more people walked near the building.

Classes were starting, another busy day on campus, and if no one else was there to do it, Peyton would make sure everyone stayed away from the building.

Soon, other staff and faculty joined her, and only when the city police and their bomb squad, complete with a bomb-sniffing German Shepherd that strained on his leash, arrived did a Mount Laguna officer make his way toward her.

"Ma'am?" The officer spoke at her shoulder, and Peyton swirled around. "We have police and the bomb squad here now to keep people away. Will you step away? Follow this officer?"

"Yeah. You need to know the box was delivered to my office. This is my fault! And an officer is still in the building!"

A female officer stepped forward and took her shoulder, escorting a panicked Peyton in the direction of the grassy quad, far away from the Winters Building. The campus had become a scene of chaos, with students and faculty trying to watch while staying as far away as possible while police, the bomb squad, and fire trucks rolled onto campus.

"Ma'am? Hi. My name is Officer Cardoza. First, this is not your fault. Second, we know about the officer. Please come with me. I'd like to get your statement."

Peyton tried to focus on the officer, but she couldn't take her eyes off the office door. Why hadn't Mateo come out yet? Where was he? What if the bomb went off and he was still in the building?

"Ma'am?" the officer asked again.

"Oh yeah, right. Sorry. What did you ask?"

The tall, brown-haired officer pulled out a notepad and a pen. "What can you tell me about the box? Did you see who delivered it?"

Peyton shook her head. She felt so useless here. Was this bomb threat done by the same people who'd prank-called her and dumped the water on her? Was this all because she was a lowly cog in the government? If they believed acting out against her would change anything, she pitied them. All this effort and attacking her wouldn't get them anywhere.

"Ma'am?" the officer asked again.

Focus, Peyton, she chastised herself.

"Sorry. Sorry. Right, the box. Um, it had my name on it, printed on a plain label. I don't think it was mailed. I don't think I saw any mailing stuff, like those post office print out labels or scan codes for shipping." She closed her eyes, trying to picture the box as it had sat right outside her office door. "Nope, just the address label."

Officer Cardoza wrote it all down. "And did you see anyone in the building? Or around it?"

"No, it was already unlocked, which is weird. Usually, I'm the first one in and it's locked, unless campus security unlocks it first. Most classes in that building are offices or seminars and those don't start until closer to ten. But it was unlocked. I didn't see anyone in the building —"

Then she paused.

No, not in the building, but someone did rush by her *outside* the building.

"Ma'am?"

"There was a guy," Peyton said slowly. "He rushed past me when Mateo pushed me out of the building."

"Mateo?" the officer asked.

"Officer Rivera, MLC campus police. He walked me to my office."

"Did Officer Rivera see this guy?"

"No, no, I don't think so. Officer Rivera was in the building, making sure it was empty."

Scratch, scratch. Officer Cardoza wrote quickly.

"And the guy. Did you see what he looked like?"

Peyton closed her eyes again. Not much, not like seeing the box.

"I only caught a glimpse of him as I left the building. I didn't even register it. I thought it was a student rushing to class, and I was relieved he didn't come close to the Winters building. Then other students came near the door. My focus was on them."

"Do you recall anything about the man that you glimpsed?"

"He was wearing black. Shirt and pants, black. And a hat? Maybe a backwards ball cap? That's all I have."

Cardoza wrote that down as well, then gave Peyton a tight smile.

"Well, campus police have cameras all around, and if he brought a box to campus, he probably drove, so we'll get the parking lot cameras as well. The fact we have an idea of what he might be wearing helps us figure out who to keep an eye out for."

Officer Cardoza held out her hand. Peyton took it and they shook.

"Thank you for all this. Now, don't worry. It seems like the bomb squad has it all under control. They've probably had Officer Rivera come out of the building, and with any luck, they've already disposed of the bomb, if it was one to begin with."

Peyton nodded as the officer strode off. Her words were meant to relieve Peyton, but she wouldn't be relieved until Mateo was by her side and this whole ordeal was over.

Peyton didn't have to wait long. Like a navy-blue ship in a sea of colors, Mateo was threading his way through the chaotic throng of people and first responders, and a wash of warm relief flooded every part of her body. Her knees went weak as he neared. The tension in Mateo's body was palatable, as his jaw set with determination to locate her in the crowd. When he finally reached her, he didn't pause to speak. He wrapped his arms around her and kissed her hard. Heat radiated off his skin, whether from tension or anger, Peyton didn't care. Mateo was here, solid and real in her arms and away from danger.

"What happened?" she asked as he lifted his head and pulled her close to his chest.

"I need to find Green before I do anything else, but I had to find you first, let you know I was okay. Make sure you were okay. The bomb was made to look real, it had all the parts, but it wasn't constructed correctly. The dog sniffed it out and signaled, but when the bomb squad came in, they could see it was defective. We dodged it with this one."

A real bomb. Defective or not, someone tried to bomb her office. Bomb her. Bomb students. None it of it made any sense, and she said as much to Mateo.

"Why? Why would someone do this?"

"People like this, Peyton, they aren't thinking the way you and I do. They aren't rational. To them, bombing your office, harassing you, made sense to them. I still think it's because you are a government entity on campus, and someone doesn't like it. Mount Laguna city police think so, too, and the local branch of the FBI agrees. They showed up as the bomb squad finished."

"Do I have to worry more? Like, will this happen again?" Her voice rose slightly with the question. Mateo squeezed his arms to reassure her.

"I don't think so. There's a camera right outside the main door to the Winters building, so I'm sure we have him on video somewhere. And we will be on heightened security for the rest of the semester."

He flicked his eyes around the crowd, as if he were searching for someone. Then he grasped her elbow.

"Come on. Let's go to my office. I need to find Green. The cops and FBI have been asking if we got a bomb threat this morning or if we saw anything on the screens. I didn't take any calls, but I wasn't in the one in the office. Green was. At least, he was supposed to be. I want to question him before anyone else gets to him."

Peyton took a long stride to keep up with him. "Why before anyone else?"

Mateo's lips thinned as they approached the campus police office. "Because if there was a threat or someone on video, I know why he missed it. And that's his third strike."

"Green! Where the fuck are you?" Mateo's bellowing voice carried throughout the office.

Never in his life had Mateo felt such burning fury at another person, and he had a knock-about younger brother who had caused him lifelong strife. But nothing Damon had ever done came close to Green dropping the ball this hard.

This was something deeper. Something raw. Something unforgivable.

If Mateo were right, then Green's actions could have led to Peyton getting hurt or worse. Peyton was *his*, and there was no way in hell he'd let Green get away with this level of fuckery.

Too bad if Green lost his job, fuck him and his police career. He didn't deserve the job if he couldn't do it.

Officer Aaron Green stepped around a padded office divider, as though he'd been hiding behind it. All this chaos, the fucking bomb squad on campus, city police and FBI, and he was hiding in the office?

Fuck him. Mateo was done with Green.

"What the hell, Green? Do you have any idea what's going on today? And you're hiding out here? What is *wrong* with you?"

With a slight push of his hand, Mateo set Peyton behind him, shielding her again with his body. Mateo didn't know how Green would react, especially if he'd been drinking and there was a good chance Mateo was going to get him fired today.

Green didn't have to get close enough for Mateo to smell it. Even over his own sweat and the general scent of panic that permeated the entire campus, the odor of rotting whiskey hung thick on Green.

How much did that man have to drink that morning?

Then Mateo let his eyes scan over Green — his disheveled uniform, his mussed hair, the bags under his eyes, and Mateo knew. Green hadn't been drinking this morning. No, he was still drinking from last night.

Fuck.

This was worse than he thought.

"What? I thought someone should stay here and hold down the fort."

Pathetic excuse.

"Really? When all hell is breaking loose and police are needed more than ever, you hide out here? And what kind of work were you doing? Because the FBI is going to want to know if any bomb threats were called in or if we have video of the guy leaving the fucking bomb. I wasn't in the office, Green. *You* were on the clock, so that leaves you. Did we get a bomb threat? Anything on the videos? Did you see anyone around campus this morning? Or hell, last night, because it sure as fuck looks like you slept here."

Green opened and closed his mouth like a fish on land.

Of course, he had no answer.

Green's eyes flicked to the office phone where a red light blinked steadily.

A message on the phone.

Mateo was ready to explode.

Glaring at Green, Mateo stormed over to the table on which the phone sat, and keeping his eyes locked on Green, pushed the message button then the speaker button.

"*We are the righteous anarchists. We know the fascist government has been working on the MLC campus, using student resources to keep us oppressed. Don't be surprised when you get a big bang from us this morning.*"

Click.

The furious rumbling that coursed through Mateo was boundless, and in a split second he made a choice. He leapt over the table in a shockingly swift movement, so fast his own brain couldn't keep up with his body that seemed to be on autopilot, and he was in Green's face. He grabbed the front of Green's uniform and slammed him into the wall.

"You could have killed her, you dumb fuck! You could have killed students! What is wrong with you?"

"Mateo!"

A light voice managed to seep into the fury-ridden fog of his brain, and slowly Mateo calmed himself, releasing his hold on Green.

If he hadn't, he was certain he would have killed Aaron.

He gave Green another quick shove before he stepped away, closer to Peyton. The anger still roiled, but keeping his focus on Peyton helped him rein it in.

Green was going to lose his job. It didn't serve anyone if Mateo lost his as well. The danger was over, Peyton was fine, the campus intact. Time to focus on what would happen next.

"Officer Rivera, the Mount Laguna police, and the FBI are here. What do we have for them?"

President Anderson stood in the doorway, as imposing as she could muster with her petite frame, her hands clenched into fists at her sides, and two men flanking her. One wore a gray suit, the other a blue uniform, much like Mateo's. FBI and Mount Laguna city police.

"Crimson, good to see you," Mateo stepped around Peyton and shook the man's hand.

"What do you have for us?" Crimson asked.

Mateo laid out everything they knew, then queued up the videos from that morning, explaining he hadn't seen them yet. Dozens of police and FBI officers crowded into the small office for the non-traditional debriefing and security scan.

The man in black that Peyton had described was found on one of the videos carrying a box from his car. The license plate was clearly visible on the camera, as was the lack of a parking sticker. Mateo also played the phone recording for them, and Crimson asked that Mateo send all the information to the Mount Laguna police station. The FBI and the police were going to take over the case from here.

Green had sagely kept quiet, trying to make himself as small as possible at the rear of the office.

But Mateo didn't forget about him. Once most of the officers cleared out, President Anderson remained behind with several other staff members from her office.

"Are you sure you're okay, Peyton? This isn't going to set your research or findings behind, will it?" Anderson asked.

Peyton shook her head. "No. Nothing happened to the office. My laptop is fine. I'm fine. This was just unexpected," she waved her hand in the air to suggest everything that had happened that day. "But now that the cops have everything they need to catch this guy, we can get back to work."

Dr. Anderson flicked her eyes to Mateo. "Do you think we'll have any more incidents?"

Mateo squinted for a moment, considering his answer before he spoke. "I don't think so. A lot of times with groups like these, it's a ringleader who keeps everyone involved. If this guy is the ringleader, or rats out the ringleader, the rest of the group will fade out. I think you'll see the vandalism on campus cools after today."

Dr. Anderson flicked her weary gaze from Mateo to Peyton and back. "Okay, I think that's everything. A lot of paperwork for all of us, but we're all fine, and that's all that matters."

Mateo lifted his hand to interrupt her and turned to Peyton. "Can you excuse us for a minute?"

Peyton nodded. She understood what he needed to tell the president of the college and most likely was glad to be absent for that conversation. She exited the office and headed toward the Winters building to see if her office was cleared.

Once Peyton's backside disappeared from the door frame, Mateo focused on the president. "We have a problem."

Mateo expected the unnaturally silent Green to protest, to interrupt. Instead, the man sat in a hung-over stupor on a folding chair, awaiting his fate. Mateo shook his head in disappointment and tugged at his uniform vest.

"What problem?" Dr. Anderson asked, her worry lines etching deeper into her face.

"It's Officer Green," Mateo said as he lowered his voice. Aaron might know Mateo was reporting him, but it didn't make it any easier to hear one's sins broadcasted aloud. "He's had a drinking problem as of late. He covered it well, but he'd come to campus drunk a few times, and I called him on it. He stopped, so I thought he'd gotten help and we were done with it. Today, though, he was drunk when I came to campus, and it appears that he missed the bomb threat and the video surveillance. He also stayed in the office while we dealt with the bomb squad."

Dr. Anderson raised a thin, graying eyebrow at the dejected-looking man on the far side of the room.

"Is that right?" Then she huffed out an exasperated breath. "You covered for him?"

Mateo pursed his lips and shrugged slightly. "Not really covered. I told him to not to come to campus while drinking, get help with AA or something, and if he did that, I wouldn't report it. And he did all that until today. So now I'm reporting it."

Dr. Anderson rubbed her forehead. Mateo couldn't imagine the nightmare she had to deal with over the bomb scare, and now to be forced to deal with an errant security officer? Her bad day was only getting worse, and Mateo didn't envy her load of upcoming paperwork.

"Okay. Do me a favor. Relieve him of duty. Get his weapons, his shield, and his keys. He's on suspension until we can complete our internal investigation. The chancellors will have to be apprised of this before we can do anything officially. And they will have a lot of questions for you. Got it?"

For a tiny woman, she spoke and behaved like a colonel in an army. Mateo guessed she'd have to, running an entire college.

"Yes, ma'am," he agreed, and she spun around, leaving him with Green. "Did you hear her?" Mateo asked without looking at Aaron.

Green didn't answer. Instead, Mateo heard the sound of Green's belt, shield, and keys hitting the table with a *clunk* as he left them behind. Then he walked out the door without giving Mateo a backward glance.

Fucker, Mateo thought as President Anderson followed Green out the door. Then he turned to assess the upturned office, moved the table back against the wall, and settled into the computer near the front of the office. His first task would be to call Cortes in for some overtime now that Green was on suspension.

Then he'd have to begin writing his reports. It looked like Mateo was going to be working overtime, too. What a miserable day.

But not too long. He'd already promised himself that he'd head over to Peyton's office before she left for home.

Chapter Thirteen

PEYTON COULDN'T FOCUS on any of her work for the rest of the day. She'd already called Jada and told her to stay home, unless she had classes, then go only to classes and right back home.

"Is everything okay?" she had asked Peyton, her concern pouring from the phone. "Are you okay?"

What an amazing assistant, Peyton thought to herself. She was going to miss Jada terribly when she left. She made a mental note to let Jada know that if she ever needed a letter of recommendation or a job to contact her.

"We had a bomb threat, but things are calming down. I'd rather have you safe."

"Holy cow! I heard something was going on at campus, but not a bomb threat! Okay. I'll take the time to start getting ready for finals. That should keep me busy."

"Be safe, Jada, and I'll see you next week."

"No more campus visits?" Jada asked.

Peyton glanced at the cursed calendar on her desk. The days were mostly empty. Only a few more weeks and her time down here was done. Even after the chaos of today, that prospect, knowing she'd have to say goodbye to Mateo, weighed on her.

"No, no more," Peyton told her. "We're just compiling notes and numbers and getting the reports and presentations ready."

"Who are you delivering this to, anyway?"

Peyton loved Jada's curiosity. "The Superintendent of Public Instruction and his team. We are combining it with all the northern and central California updates to determine funding and allocation of resources for the next ten years."

"Numbers and presentations, ugh," Jada commented lightly. "Well, be safe on campus. Make sure Officer Rivera takes care of you. No more trouble, okay?"

Peyton smiled into the phone. "I promise. See you next week."

She hung up the phone and logged into her laptop. Time to lose herself in work so she could forget about this odious, tiring day and go home as soon as possible. All she wanted to do was get in her sweats and curl up on the couch with Mateo.

Dr. Anderson sent her an email later in the day, checking up on her. *Thoughtful*, Peyton mused, emailing her back.

Before she knew it, Mateo was knocking on her office door frame.

"Hey, beautiful. Are you ready to go?"

The day had passed quickly once she had thrown herself into her notes. Closing her laptop, she let her gaze wander over his body. He looked so weary, so beaten down by the day, she longed to kiss his trauma away. His normally sun-kissed bronzed skin was sallow, and while his sunglasses hid his eyes, she was certain they'd have bags under them. Her heart broke. This day had been the worst — he had risked his life to keep her safe, dealt with a possible bomb, coordinated with city police and FBI, and then, to top it all off, reported a fellow officer for on-the-job drinking. She'd ask him about *that* later.

It made her day of crunching numbers seem so insignificant in comparison.

And soon she'd have to tell him goodbye. Just another hit to the end of the semester.

But he'd stolen her heart like a thief in the night. How could she leave her heart?

"Yeah, I'm ready," she answered in a tight voice, grabbing her bag behind her chair. She slipped her laptop and notebook into it, grabbed her purse, then walked toward the door.

She stopped right in front of him, taking a moment to lay her hand on his chest, as if to prove to herself that he was there, that he was real. The rough fabric of his uniform brushed against her fingers, moving steadily with each breath he took. He was real. He was here.

"You don't have to take me home," she told him.

She lifted her face to his and kissed him softly. It seemed like he needed it, and his body relaxed, melting into hers before he pulled his lips away.

"I do. If not for you, then for me. Just in case, but I won't have you walking alone to your car or your apartment, not after today. I'll stay the night, then bring you back tomorrow morning. For the next few weeks, you have your own personal security."

Peyton had no words and gave him a weak smile. Mateo took her hand, threading his thick fingers with hers, and walked her to her car.

"I'm sorry, by the way," she said hesitantly.

The guilt she felt about the violence on campus culminating that morning was something she'd managed to push to the back of her mind. But now that he was walking next to her, a silent sentinel in the late afternoon, the impact of that guilt returned.

"Sorry? For what?" His eyes focused on the parking lot, most likely searching for anyone who didn't fit on campus, Peyton presumed.

"For what happened today. I had no idea that my being here on campus would cause all these problems."

Peyton kept walking, but Mateo stopped and jerked her hand back.

"Wait, what?" he asked.

"This is all my fault. If that bomb had been real, you or any of the students or staff could have been killed."

Her eyes watered, and she couldn't bring herself to look at him as she confessed her guilt. Mateo uttered a gruff breath and wrapped his arms around her, clasping her tightly to his chest.

"Hey, babe, none of today was your fault," his voice a low rumble in her ear. "Extremists find any excuse, any outlet, and you were convenient. If not you, they would've focused on someone else on campus, and then we might not have caught it. As for the danger today, that's not on you. That's on Officer Green and him alone. He should have been sober enough to do his job, catch either the bomb threat or the video, and take appropriate action. Do *not* put that on yourself."

Peyton rested her head on his chest, letting herself be lulled by his words. Maybe he was right. Maybe she wasn't at fault. None of it made her feel any better.

She rubbed her cheek against his uniform. "You blocked me from the box. You put your body in front of that bomb for me. Why did you do that?"

It seemed a stupid question, one her heart knew the answer to, but she couldn't bring her mind to accept it.

His arms tightened around her. "Because I love you, and I'd give my life to protect yours at all costs. Because the thought of losing you is something I can't bring myself to bear."

Peyton wiped her watery eyes on Mateo's uniform before lifting her lips to his and kissing him again, using her mouth to tell him that yes, she understood, and yes, she felt the same.

"Do you want to head to my room?" she asked.

Once Mateo got her home, he busied himself in the kitchen, making a quick dinner of spaghetti from a jar while Peyton changed into comfortable sweats. Mateo slipped off his uniform shirt and hung it on a doorknob and cooked in his plain white t-shirt. Not sexy, but comfortable and easier to relax in than his full uniform.

They ate dinner at the coffee table, and while they watched some brain-numbing TV, which Mateo thought was just what they needed, they cuddled on the couch. He kept touching her, as if to convince himself that Peyton was here next to him, to protect her from anything else that might happen.

Mateo had wanted to pounce on Peyton as soon as they got to her place. Unlike himself, who craved a physical connection after a life-endangering day, Peyton seemed reserved. Not that he blamed her. It was probably the first time her life had ever been threatened. Though it was relatively common for Mateo, this was a new experience for Peyton, and she was in a state of shock.

"Badly," he answered her question honestly. "I want to take you into your room and ravage the fuck out of you. But right now, I think you need something else, something more tame and low key."

She nodded, brushing her hair from her face. The lines on her face were still tensed, and she didn't feel fully relaxed as she reclined on him on the couch. Had the day affected her that much?

"Are you okay?" he asked, already knowing the answer.

Peyton sat up but kept her face adverted. She couldn't look at him.

That's not good, he thought.

"No. I don't think I am."

Mateo inhaled, wondering if she should have gone to the ER or counseling following the bomb scare instead of going back to work. She appeared upset and distracted but not to the point where he thought she needed help. Had he missed the mark on her coping ability?

"But it's not because of the thing today." She flapped her hand at him, unable to call it what it was. A bomb threat. "It's because it even made the news. All the major California networks carried it, as did several online outlets."

His eyebrows wrinkled together. What was wrong with the news coverage? Did someone she knew up north not know she was down here? Was she hiding something?

From the expression on her face, he knew. Peyton had no guile. She *had* to be hiding something.

"I got an email from the assistant to the Vice-Superintendent. He's my boss, essentially. And they didn't like the government spin that the news put on everything. Not that what I'm working on is top secret, but it will affect how millions of educational dollars are spent, so the information is kinda important."

A sinking sensation churned in Mateo's gut and wouldn't abate. As much as he hated to admit it, he knew exactly where this conversation was going. And he wasn't quite ready to have it yet. But here he was. And it looked like he was going to have to tell her the decision he'd made several weeks ago.

He could only hope she agreed and wanted to go along with it.

"So did your boss get in contact with you?"

Peyton nodded, her blonde hair falling into her face and hiding her eyes.

"Yeah, but not until we got home. It was on my phone while I was changing. An email."

"They want you back up north," he guessed in a flat tone.

She nodded again. "Yeah. They wanted me to leave this weekend, I told them I had to close up the office and let my apartment people know, and pack. So, I guess what I'm saying is . . ."

But she didn't say it. She let it trail off.

She didn't have to say it. It was obvious.

She was moving back up to Sacramento. Not in a few weeks but a few days.

"We knew this was coming," Mateo responded in a rough voice. His chest ached, throbbed, and he struggled to talk around it.

What if she doesn't agree? What if this is the wrong choice?

Fuck it, a small voice inside him said. *Fortune favors the brave.*

"Yeah, but I wanted more time with you," her voice dropped as she spoke, strained, and her hand reached out and grasped his, as if she needed something solid to hold on to. "I just found you and now I have to leave. I thought we'd have more time."

"Wouldn't that have made a goodbye more difficult?" he asked.

She wiped at her face with her sleeve. "I guess. But I still wanted that time."

His heart hammered in his chest, bruising it. Mateo took a deep breath and moved his hand so their fingers threaded together. He wasn't about to let her go.

"Why? Why did you want more time?"

She moved her head so she finally faced him. This was what he wanted, to be able to look her in the eyes. In her clear blue eyes.

"What? Why kind of question is that?"

"An important one. Why did you want more time?"

She tried to slip her face to the side again, but he caught her chin with his finger.

"Why?"

"I thought it was obvious. I've said it before."

"No you haven't," he told her. "You've hinted at it, but you've never said it."

Peyton rubbed her lips together.

"Yeah, but that doesn't mean my heart isn't invested, just because I haven't said it."

"So you love me?"

Now he was playing with her. The weight in his chest lifted, and he struggled not to smile.

"What about you? It's not like you've been saying it all the time."

He did laugh at that, a low chuckle deep in his throat. "Oh, I've said it, and a lot more than you. I even said it tonight. And I thought throwing myself in front of a bomb really showed you how I feel."

Her finger caressed his hand, and a slight smile tugged at her lips. "Well, a dud bomb."

"Oh, so now I don't get credit for that? We didn't know it was a dud at the time."

Peyton smiled widely now, and Mateo had a flush of gratification that she was able to find some humor in this shit day.

"Ok, you win. Yes, you did show me how much you love me by throwing yourself in front of the bomb."

"So, can you say it to me?"

She bit her lower lip before speaking. "I love you, Mateo, and I'm devastated that I have to leave."

He took her other hand in his so they faced each other fully on the couch.

"What if we could avoid that?"

Her smile fled. "I can't quit my job, Mateo. It's a great job, and I love it."

Mateo shook his head. "No. I have another idea."

"Northern California has a lot of colleges. Sacramento City College is a beautiful campus on the west side of the city."

Peyton thought her chest would explode at his words. They were not what she'd expected, and she had a moment of confusion. *Wait, he didn't want her to quit her job?*

Was he suggesting . . .? What exactly was he suggesting?

"What are you saying, Mateo?"

He leaned his earnest, handsome face in close to hers, and her breath caught in her throat.

"I love you, Peyton. I adore you and everything about you. These past five months have been amazing. I've already told Abuela, and while she's sad about it, she is also very excited for me."

"Excited for what?" Peyton breathed.

"I already contacted SCC. They had an opening for a campus police officer. I applied, and I even asked President

Anderson if she might make a recommendation for me, which she did. And they offered me a position starting in July when their new fiscal year begins. So, the only piece in this puzzle that is missing, Peyton, is you. I'm ready to pack up and move up to Sacramento with you, if you'll have me."

She froze. He was going to move north with her? He was willing to give up his job, his family and friends, his whole life here, and move north? That was. . . That was . . .

That was *amazing*.

But he still left the decision up to her. Did she want him to move up there with her? Did she love him enough for that much of a leap in their relationship? She'd said she loved him, but words were easy when they weren't permanent.

She studied Mateo's eyes, those deep, swirling black pools that showed more emotion than most men showed with their entire bodies. Those eyes that only ever looked at her with love, with intensity, with devotion.

Yes, she was ready. She did want that.

"On one condition," she told him, a light smile playing at her lips.

Mateo stiffened a bit. "What condition?"

"That when you move in, you won't get pissed if the cat ends up sleeping between us every night."

"Get twenty cats. I don't care. As long as I'm in that bed with you."

Then he kissed her and sealed their future together.

The End

And just as a reminder! If you love this book, be sure to leave a review! Reviews are life blood for authors, and I appreciate every review I receive!

Don't forget! If you want more from Michelle? Click the image below to receive three FREE short ebooks, updates, and more in your inbox!

Find the link at this website:

https://linktr.ee/mddalrympleauthor

Alluring

Look for book 4 – Alluring – coming later this year, and get ready for a flipped college stripper trope!

Craving

Excerpt from Night Shift

If you like Campus Romances by M.D Dalrymple, you'll also enjoy her police romances – The Men in Uniform Series. Take a peek at *Night Shift:*

THOSE CALLS WERE physically and mentally draining; cops worried during the entire encounter that the drug user would suffer a heart attack in custody and initiate an investigation that, on a cooler day or if the offender abused some other drug, would not happen. Fortunately, last night, no gun was found on either perp, the addicts remained upright, and the booking afterward encountered no glitches.

Matthew recalled the events, evaluating his behavior (wiping his hands on his running shorts in memory of the slimy film that covered the male offender — sometimes the sensation remained even after several showers), checking to make sure he acted by the book. As both offenders were healthy and booked into jail by early morning, Matthew and his brothers in blue considered that a win.

His mind on other matters, he paid little attention as he rounded a sharp curve of the trail. Just as he congratulated himself over a well-executed arrest, a huge German Shepherd ran onto the path, tethered by a long leash. Matthew twisted to the side of the trail to avoid tripping over the dumb beast. The animal emitted one loud bark, and Matthew paused give the dog's owner a dressing down. While he did admire the dog — the animal was a perfect specimen, it could have been a show dog — his mouth, ready to confront the owner, snapped shut.

At the other end of the tethered leash stood a slender, fairly tall woman, bright running shoes extending up to firm, tanned legs. His eyes traveled up her body, over her tiny running shorts that displayed her muscular thighs, over her fitted (*beautifully fitted,* he thought) tank top, to her angular face and sleek, ebony hair pulled back in a tight, low ponytail. Matthew's chest and loins clenched simultaneously, a sensation he had not experienced for several years.

The woman reached her hand out to make sure he wasn't going to fall, and Matthew almost took it in his. Shaking his head to clear it, he snatched his hand back.

"You OK?" The woman's liquid voice asked. "Carter just rushed out. He's normally so good and stays by my side, but we haven't gone for a run in several days, and he was excited. I am so sorry."

Concern painted her face. She was rambling, and Matthew bit the inside of his lip to stop a grin.

"No, you are good. I was able to move around him. No blood, no foul."

This time Matthew smiled, and the enchanting woman before him returned the gesture in a radiant glow. Matthew fell into that smile and was lost. He didn't even know her name.

"Beautiful dog," he said, trying to keep her engaged.

Her dark eyes sparkled with pride at the poor dog sitting obediently by her side. Carter kept looking down the trail and back at his mistress, probably wondering, *why aren't we running?*

"Oh, thanks," she replied, reaching to give her good boy a pat, and the dog pressed his head against her leg. The dog obviously loved her unconditionally. Matthew just met her and understood the dog's feelings. The electricity he felt from her burned deep within him.

"May I pet him?" Matthew reached forward and placed his hand at the dog's nose when the woman nodded. "Is he a purebred?"

Her silky hair shimmered as she nodded. "Yep, a gift from my parents when I moved out. They didn't want me living by myself."

"Good choice of a dog for that," Matthew told her. "One of my buddies is in the K9 Unit and cannot stop talking about how amazing the dog is. I've seen his shepherd in action more than once, and Germans are so well trained."

"You've seen a K9 in action? Are you a cop?"

Matthew's smile widened. He loved his job, even after asinine nights like the one before, and enjoyed telling people about it.

"Yeah, out of Tustin."

"Oh, do you live near here, then? Not Tustin? Running and all?" She gestured a slender hand at his running shorts. He had a flashing thought he hoped his package looked tempting.

"Yeah, just west of the park." He held out a hand, praying it wasn't too sweaty. He knew from experience how well *that* went over. "I'm Matthew, by the way."

"Oh, I'm Rosemarie."

Start the Men In Uniform romance series with Night Shift!

A Note

As a college professor, and a former college and grad student, I have a wealth of information about college campus life at my disposal. And since I've been reading more professor-trope romances as of late, I thought to myself, *I have an inside view on this! Why am I not writing these romances for my readers?*

For this story, I explored an oft-overlooked relationship – one between staff members. The idea arose from a couple I know at a college, where the husband and wife each work in different staff positions with very little overlap. That lack of overlap alleviates some of the complications, but is not without its own issues. Especially when the two staff departments might be at odds – something I touched on in *Craving*. Plus I just love pulling characters from all the different aspects of a college campus. I think it bring Mount Laguna College to life.

I have about seven or so more books planned for the series, which will include all types of different campus relationships. And each will be a mix of sweet with a good amount of steam! The next book scheduled, *Craving*, will focus on a visiting lecturer and campus security – something fun to look forward to!

Thank you for coming along for the ride! I hope you are loving it!

Thank you to my beta and ARC readers for reviews and feedback.

I also have to thank my college friends and colleagues throughout the years who've given me fodder for my writing.

And I want to thank my family and my hubby – my real-world HEA.

About the Author

Michelle Deerwester-Dalrymple is a professor of writing and an author. She started reading when she was 3 years old, writing when she was 4, and published her first poem at age 16. She has written articles and essays on a variety of topics, including several texts on writing for middle and high school students. She is also working on a novel inspired by actual events. She lives in California with her family of seven.

You can visit her blog page, sign up for her newsletter, and follow all her socials at:
https://linktr.ee/mddalrympleauthor

Craving

Also by the Author:

As Michelle Deerwester-Dalrymple
Glen Highland Romance
The Courtship of the Glen –Prequel Short Novella
To Dance in the Glen – Book 1
The Lady of the Glen – Book 2
The Exile of the Glen – Book 3
The Jewel of the Glen – Book 4
The Seduction of the Glen – Book 5
The Warrior of the Glen – Book 6
An Echo in the Glen – Book 7
The Blackguard of the Glen – Book 8

The Celtic Highland Maidens
The Maiden of the Storm
The Maiden of the Grove
The Maiden of the Celts
The Maiden of the Stones – coming soon
The Maiden of the Loch – coming soon

Look for the Fairy Tale *Before* Series
Before the Glass Slipper
Before the Magic Mirror
Before the Cursed Beast
Before the Red Cloak
Before the Magic Lamp

<u>Historical Fevered Series – short and steamy romance</u>
The Highlander's Scarred Heart
The Highlander's Legacy
The Highlander's Return
Her Knight's Second Chance
The Highlander's Vow
Her Outlaw Highlander
Her Knight's Christmas Gift

<u>As M. D. Dalrymple: Men in Uniform Series</u>
Night Shift – Book 1
Day Shift – Book 2
Overtime – Book 3
Holiday Pay – Book 4
School Resource Officer -- Book 5
Holdover – Book 6 coming soon

<u>Campus Heat Series</u>
Charming – Book 1
Tempting – Book 2
Infatuated – Book 3
Craving – Book 4
Alluring – Book 5 -- coming soon